BLOND FAITH

MY LIST

Aunt Bets,
 These are some of my recent favorites. The "By The Bay" series has 3 of my short stories. The others have my name — wife friend "Jayne Ormerod's." She is also a

but later, there was some movement. She found the boy, "Jerry, has 3 of my dear ones - have you finished playing? Don't proceed." He is also

MY LIST

neighbor and friend.
She's inscribed
each of hers for
you. And, I have
too.
We hope you
enjoy them!
Love,
Gina

BLOND FAITH

A Blonds at the Beach Mystery

Jayne Ormerod

The characters and events portrayed in this book are fictitious. Any similarity to real persons, living or dead, is coincidental and not intended by the author.

Text copyrighted © 2014 by Jayne Ormerod
All rights reserved.
Printed in the United States of America

No part of this book may be reproduced or stored in a retrieval system or transmitted in any form by any means, electronic, mechanical, photocopying, recording, or otherwise, without the express written permission of the publisher.

Published by Bay Breeze Publishing Group, June 2014
Norfolk, VA

This book is dedicated to all of you wonderful readers of light-hearted and humorous cozies.

Thank you.

Acknowledgements

This is the part most every reader skips, unless they are looking for their own name to appear, so for those of you looking, here we go:

I would not be where I am were it not for the support, encouragement and friendship of my critique partners for lo these past 14 years, Sandra Brown Rarey and Eliza Fleetwood.
You two are the greatest!!!

Next, this manuscript never would have been finished were it not for the Coronado Rebel Writers, aka Krystee Kott, Julia Roller and Carrie Keyes. Thanks to you it has a much better ending.

Mystery by the Sea, the southeastern Virginia chapter of Sisters in Crime, has been there for me every step of the way, to include attending book signings and helping with the promotion.
Your support and encouragement has been invaluable.

And no good book goes unedited, so special thanks to my first final reader, Beate Boeker; my second final reader and grammar checker R. G. Koepf. (who, in turn, gives full credit of her mastery of the written word to her English teacher Helen Onderdonk.); and my third final reader Gina Buzby. Everything's fixed up right now, I hope!

My sister, Jennifer Evans, gets credit for the cover concept, and San Coils worked her magic and turned the concept into the fabulous work of art. You can see more of San's work at www.coverkicks.com

And I wouldn't even be thanking friends were it not for the constant love and support of my family. Thank you, guys!

Chapter One

"RUN!"

The command was redundant, as the sound of a gunshot had been a sufficient catalyst to get me galumphing down the dark paneled hallway faster than a speeding bullet. That was my plan, anyway.

My stocking feet slipped against the waxed floor as I adopted a speed skater's posture--my right foot sliding out and my body leaning far enough to the left that my fingers trailed on the ground--for a tight turn around the corner. A few steps later I found traction on the commercial-grade carpet of the vestibule and hit Mach One in less than six feet. Amazing what a huge dose of adrenaline can do for an overweight 48-year-old woman with bad knees.

The gunshot blast still echoed in my head, which seemed to keep the adrenaline valve wide open, which kept me moving faster than I'd ever moved in my entire life. One more tight turn and I saw sunshine pouring through the arched entryway, whose doors had been pushed open to invite sinners and saints alike to enter the hallowed halls of the Braddocks Beach Church of Divine Spiritual Enlightenment. I didn't want to get in. My goal was to get out. Arms and knees pumping, I headed for the light.

BAM! I slammed into something. Or, more accurately, someone. I bounced backwards and landed on my tailbone. Momentum pushed my skull until it cracked against the floor and then propelled my legs over my head as I completed an

1

undignified fish flop. I came to rest spread eagle on my stomach, sucking in air like a Hoover slurping up coins from the crevices of a sofa.

"Call nine-one-one!" A booming voice reverberated off the walls and roughhewn rafters high above my head. In all my years of waiting for a message from God, that wasn't what I'd expected to hear.

"God damn it," the voice echoed overhead.

Maybe that wasn't God speaking to me after all.

"Ellery, where are you? I could use your help in here." I identified the booming voice as belonging to Samantha Rose Greene, the woman I'd inherited as a neighbor. My dearly departed Aunt Izzy had left me a house filled with family heirlooms, a bank account flowing with cash, and Sam, the bossiest busybody to ever walk the earth.

"Ellery Elizabeth Tinsdale, for gawd's sake, call nine-one-one," Sam ordered again. "The reverend's been shot."

The reminder of a gun--or more importantly somebody shooting a gun--had me off the ground and running for my life again. I'd been on the business end of a gun once, and that was one too many times for me. I have made my personal paradigm to stay away from all deadly weapons, no matter which side I was on.

With a leap normally reserved for the Bolshoi, I soared over the man spread eagle on the floor, taking scant notice of the bloody face and nose freshly torqued at an unnatural angle, the laws of gross tonnage having worked in my favor. The EMTs could take care of him, too. They're trained to deal with blood. My genetic coding has me faint at the mere prospect.

With nary a backward glance, I raced out the door at a pace I hoped was faster than a speeding bullet and bee-lined it towards the nearest building, the Catholic Church across the street.

Once inside, I scampered up one flight of cement steps,

barged into the office, grabbed the phone out of a surprised secretary's hand and did just as Sam had instructed--called 9-1-1. Or tried to, anyway. You'd think it would have been an easy enough thing to do, but with my fingers shaking the way they were and my heart pounding the way it was and my mind shooting off in as many directions as a 4th of July fireworks display, it took a few tries.

"Nine-one-one. What's your emergency?"

"Reverend Hammersmith's been shot. He's at the Church of Divine Spiritual Enlightenment on Cowpens Street," I said, the words tumbling out in one long stream. Voicing the event made it more real, and that sent a tsunami-size wave of horror washing through my body, which effectively rinsed away all of the adrenaline that had kept me going. My legs gave out and I sank to the floor in a jumbled heap on the commercial-grade Berber.

A chorus of gasps erupted from the small crowd that had gathered around while I'd been trying to place the phone call. That was followed by a clatter of feet as they raced *en masse*—not to offer aid to my crumpled self, but to look out the window that faced the scene of the crime.

"Your name please?" the operator asked.

"Ellery Tinsdale. And please hurry. Before someone else gets shot."

"Ma'am, are you saying a gunman is on the loose?" the 9-1-1 operator asked.

"Yes," I yelled as I tried to wrap my mouth around the words to explain what little I could piece together of the events: the reverend had been shot by a crazed lunatic wandering the halls armed with an Uzi, a sawed off shotgun and a battery of small caliber pistols strapped to his torso. At least that's how I pictured the scene in my mind's eye. But had that really been what had happened? "Maybe. I don't know. All I heard was one gunshot."

I drew a deep breath then started to speak in what I hoped was a coherent manner. "Samantha Greene and I were in the hallways when we heard a gun go off. She ran to see what happened, found the reverend and yelled to me, 'Call nine-one-one! The reverend's been shot!'"

The sound of approaching sirens let me know the emergency operator had sent help, bless her ever lovin' soul. I dropped the phone, hauled myself up off the floor and raced to the window to watch the goings on for myself. With my height of just a skosh over six feet, I didn't have any trouble peering over the heads of the shorter women in front of me.

We watched in total--and slightly unnerving--silence as the four police cars screeched to a halt in the drop-off lane in front of the church. Three fire trucks and a lone ambulance followed in their wake. Like some well-choreographed *Dancing with the Stars* ensemble performance, they assembled their gear and charged through the front door. As expected, a gaggle of looky loos quickly formed on the sidewalk below. I sometimes wonder if the entire village is tied into the 9-1-1 dispatch center as entire regiments of nosy bodies swarm within a minute of any emergency, oftentimes arriving on the scene before the police do.

"This is gonna be big," a squatty woman in front of me said. Without another word, the entire group of office personnel and TMVs--Thursday Morning Volunteers--turned and, shoving and pushing me out of the way like I was yesterday's tater tots, headed out the door and clattered down the stairs.

I could follow them and join the crowd standing in the sweltering heat to wait for word on Reverend Hammersmith's injuries, or I could pull an executive leather desk chair over to the window and wait in solitude and air-conditioning for word on Reverend Hammersmith's injuries. Going home was not an option because my shoes had been lost somewhere in the church and I wasn't about to walk the five blocks across town in my stocking feet.

Once comfortably ensconced in a big chair, I watched the activity below with interest, but with curious thoughts running through my mind. What are the odds of a crazed gunman roaming the halls of a church? On a Thursday? At lunch hour? Usually the place is completely empty. Which is why Sam and I had chosen that time to go there. Don't those deranged individuals usually want a larger venue? In a larger town? I sighed, as the facts registered. Crazed gunman indeed. No doubt something unusual had happened, but nothing on the scale of my worst fears. The reverend hadn't been injured too badly. The EMTs would issue a band aid and we'd all have a good laugh at my tendency to exaggerate a situation.

"Ms. Tinsdale."

I jumped clean out of my chair at the sound of a deep male voice. Turning, I looked towards the doorway and saw Officer Glenn, Braddocks Beach beat cop, standing there. He's a tall drink of water, as my southern momma used to say. Usually all business, he was more serious now than I'd ever seen him. So serious in fact, it gave me the heebie jeebies.

"I'm here to take you over to see Chief Lewis," he said. "He has a few questions for you about, you know." Officer Glen tipped his head in the general direction of the activity across the street.

Uh oh. What if the new chief asked me why I was in the church in the first place? I didn't want to lie to a police officer, but I didn't want to tell him the truth, either. Was there any way to put a positive spin on the fact that we'd intended to steal a key from the church secretary's desk in order to steal a key from the Reverend's desk in order to break into my family's secret files locked in the church's basement?

"Now, Ms. Tinsdale." Officer Glen jerked his left thumb in the direction of the exit while slipping his right one until it rested on the butt of his Glock.

Far be it from me to argue with a man with a gun.

He escorted me--with a gentle but firm hold on my elbow--down the stairs, out the door and across the street where the crowds parted for us like the waters had parted for Moses. I couldn't help but notice the solemnity of the crowd. Something was wrong. Very wrong.

Officer Glen steered me into the church and past the scene of the crime, which was abuzz with activity, and down to the well-appointed-but-not-too-fussy community room where the newly appointed Police Chief Lewis waited. If it weren't for his police uniform of crisp white shirt, dark blue pants, steel toed black boots and gun strapped around his waist, I wouldn't have recognized him. The man didn't look anything like the Glamour Shots picture they'd run in the Braddocks Beach Bugle upon his arrival in town last week. In person, this man seemed too round, too sloppy, and, with skin the color that reminded me of a fish's underbelly, too pale. Worse, he also appeared too accusatory. I didn't like him on sight.

"Where are your shoes?" the chief asked without benefit of niceties.

"Last I checked, going shoeless is not illegal in this town." Truth be told, Sam had made me take off my mules so that their slap-slapping sound wouldn't announce our arrival when we broke into the church office. And in all of the hullabaloo after the shooting, I had no idea where my shoes were. I walked across the room and settled into a low-slung overstuffed chair. It was snow white. I was dressed in all black. So much for my hopes of blending into my environment.

"Ms. Tinsdale," the Chief said as he turned to face me. "A man has been brutally murdered not fifty feet from where you sit. I am charged with protecting the citizens of this town, and in order to do that I need to find out who killed Reverend John Thomas Hammersmith, and I don't have time to play games. Now, I'll ask again, where are your shoes?"

"Reverend Hammersmith was mur...mur...mur..." I

couldn't say the word. My brain didn't seem capable of wrapping itself around the idea. Sam had said he'd shot himself, as in an accident, not dead by way of murder!

"Yes, and according to Ms. Greene, you were in the church when it happened. That makes you a viable witness. So I'll ask again, where are your shoes?"

The way Chief Lewis focused his beady eyes on me, I got the crazy feeling that my being in the church also made me a viable suspect. High up there on my list of things I don't like is being on the short list of possible killers. Sad as it may seem, I know this from experience.

"Ms. Tinsdale. Your shoes?" Chief Lewis stared at me in a way I found very intimidating.

Chief Lewis appeared to be from the "Guilty until proven innocent" school of thought and my self-preservation instincts kicked into high gear. "Was Reverend Hammersmith killed with one of my shoes?"

"No."

"Then my shoes have no bearing on this case."

"Okay then. Let's try this again." The Chief stopped his pacing right in front of me, locked his legs shoulder-width apart, tucked his hands under opposite armpits, and glared down at me. The dark recesses of his nostrils reminded me of a recent encounter I'd had with a Glock, where I'd not been on the preferred trigger-pulling side. I shook off the haunting memory the way a dog shakes off soap suds.

"What business brought you to the church today?"

I spied a tin of butter cookies sitting on the antique Pembroke table next to my chair. Chocolate was my usual go-to comfort food, but rich, crunchy, crunchy, buttery goodness would do in a pinch, and I needed a whole lot of comfort right now, what with trying *not* to think about Reverend Hammersmith's murder and *not* kowtowing to the chief's inquisition. I reached for a stack, stuffed three in my mouth and chewed thoughtfully, using the seconds to compose my response. What would a good lawyer advise? It's times like this that TMT (too much television) pays off.

After a great show of swallowing, I said, "I'm invoking my rights under the Fifth Amendment to not answer that question."

Chief Lewis blew out an exasperated breath while scrubbing his five o'clock shadow--which was four hours early--between his hands. He turned and spoke to the scrawny cop guarding the double French doors. "Why me?"

The cop shrugged.

Chief Lewis turned back to me. "Where were you when you heard a gun being fired?" he tried again. His manner of speaking reminded me of the Tin Man in the Wizard of Oz before Dorothy oiled his jaw hinge.

"I take the fifth."

"Did you even hear a gunshot?"

"The fifth."

"Know what I think?" The chief dropped his hands so they rested on either arm of my chair, bringing our noses to within Eskimo-kissing distance and giving me a whiff of his coffee breath. "I think you killed Reverend Hammersmith."

"No," I responded with all the indignity I could muster. "Of course I didn't. He killed himself."

The chief's eyes narrowed to accusatory slits. "And how do you know that?"

Because Sam said so, I thought. But that didn't sound like the most prudent of answers at this point. It might make her look like a murderer and me an abettor. I did my best goldfish imitation, my mouth opening and closing with no words actually coming out.

Chief Lewis stood and resumed pacing in ever-shrinking circles around my chair. His snake-eyed gaze never wandered from me. His fingers tapped out a soft staccato against the butt of his gun in the unsettling manner of *The Telltale Heart*. "Let's try this again. What were you doing in the church?"

I sat up straighter, squared my shoulders and looked Chief Lewis right in his stony gray eyes. I didn't like this guy. Not in the least. And I didn't want to talk with him anymore, lest my tongue slip, landing both Sam and I in jail. "Last I checked there wasn't anything illegal about having a personal crisis of faith, which, unless you are an ordained minister, I have no compulsion to share with you. Now, if you'll excuse me..." It was a struggle, but I managed to get myself out of the low chair and prepared to make a grand exit.

But before I could escape the room, Chief Lewis got in the last words. "I'm a good cop. And a good cop *always* gets his man. Or woman, as the case may be."

Chapter Two

If you've ever been accused of a crime, you know the first thing to be done is talk to a lawyer. So that's where I headed without further ado. And also without shoes. I honestly had no idea where they were.

My lungs and knees were pushed beyond their comfort zones—and I'm the first to admit the threshold on that is very low--as I skedaddled across Quebec Street and scurried beneath the canopy of buckeye trees lining Cowpens Street. According to urban legend, Braddocks Beach's founding fathers Charles Braddock and my own relative Frederick Tinsdale named all the streets in the grid that made up the residential neighborhood area of the town in honor of significant Revolutionary War battles. I had no idea what, or where, a Cowpens was, though.

A right turn on Lexington brought me to the shopping district, aka Tourist Central, which consisted of a circle of false-fronted Victorian shops accessed by a one-way street called Tinsdale Circle. Yeah, I'm related. Frederick was my seven-times great-grandfather, a fact I didn't know until a few weeks ago. It's a really weird thing to have a street named after you, but I digress.

In the center of Tinsdale Circle was Tinsdale Park, a large green space complete with rustic gazebo. The park hosted community concerts every Saturday night in the summertime. This offered yet another excuse for a community potluck picnic. There are a lot of things I love about this town, and community potlucks top my list.

Lexington Street runs north and south and Ticonderoga

Street runs east and west out of town. At the very southern tip of it all is beautiful Lake Braddock, boasting 39,000 acres of crystal clear water, over a hundred miles of shoreline, and a marina of sail, paddle and small motor boats to enable residents and tourists alike to enjoy a day on the water. What makes it all so beautiful is that other than the town and its grand old hotel, the rest of the shoreline remains relatively undeveloped. Oh, there are a few remote hunting and fishing cabins, but as yet none of the land owners have sold out to a real estate developer, tempting as the offers may be.

I kept walking along Tinsdale Circle, dodging the tourists that flocked to Braddocks Beach for a change from the hustle and bustle of the city. It's not so much a change in geography as a change in time periods. Braddocks Beach seemed to be stuck in the 1950s, and the people worked hard to keep it that way.

My attorney's office is on the southwestern arc of Tinsdale Circle, above Mason's Tack and Saddlery. As I climbed the narrow, musty, squeaky steps, I collected my thoughts. How was I going to tell Max I'd just been accused of murder? Again.

"Hello, Merry Sue," I said to Max's perpetually cheerful legal secretary who sat perched on her chair behind a big computer screen.

"Good morning, Ms. Tinsdale," Merry Sue said in her whispery voice that seemed more appropriate for a phone sex operator than a legal secretary. But her provocative voice belied her Plain Jane appearance. She was the poster child for "unremarkable," with thin, limp brown hair and washed out grey eyes. It didn't help that she always dressed in her grandmother's cast off cardigans and A-line skirts. And where she found penny loafers in this age of stilettos, I'll never know. But Merry Sue had a great personality and was as sharp as any legal secretary I'd ever met.

"I was just going to call you, and here you are," she said.

"Did you need me to sign some more papers or

something?" Never in my life had I signed so many papers, but never in my life had I inherited such a vast assortment of cash, stocks, businesses, real estate holdings, antiques and who knew what else. Technically, though, I hadn't inherited anything, and wouldn't for four years and eleven months, a secret known only to Max and myself at this point. And only then, if I spent every waking and sleeping second of my life within a 100-mile radius of the town's limits. Max told me Aunt Izzy had hoped I'd learn to love living here and not take the millions and run.

But I wouldn't be inheriting anything if I were convicted of murder, on account of the nearest woman's penitentiary was down by Marysville, about a hundred and fifty miles away. Focusing all my energy on the task at hand, I asked, "Is Max available?"

"He sure is. He needs to talk finances with you."

"Finances?" Uh-oh.

"Max needs to know what your plans are for meeting current expenses, which are adding up."

Double uh-oh. I had arrived in Braddocks Beach last month with a whopping $169 to my name and no employment prospects in sight as I was a teacher certified in the state of Virginia, not Ohio, and the two did not share reciprocity. Not that it mattered because there were no teaching jobs in the area anyway. Thankfully, the terms of Aunt Izzy's will covered the basic necessities of life (food, clothing and shelter) for the duration of my time in Braddocks Beach, so it's not like I would ever starve to death.

Without cash on hand though, I'd developed a horrible habit of telling local merchants to "Just put that on my tab and send it over to Max." I hated to think about how much I'd spent. A lot. A whole heaping lot. And on things that might not technically fit into even the broadest interpretation of the food/clothing/shelter allowances. The last thing I wanted to do was discuss my precarious financial position with Max.

Before I could beat a hasty retreat, the inner office door opened. "Merry Sue, I'm going...oh, Ellery..." Geoffrey Maxamillian Eddington III did not live up to his grand name. A twenty-something man of slight stature, he wore a blue pinstripe suit that was two sizes too big for him. Maybe he planned to grow into it. Max was thrifty that way.

He approached me with a wary look in his eyes. "Hello, Ellery."

"Max." I offered my most dazzling Queen Bee smile.

The corner of Max's mouth lifted ever so slightly in return. Not a good sign.

"Max," Merry Sue interrupted. "You wanted me to remind you to remind Ms. Tinsdale about the property."

"Yes. Thank you." Max turned toward me. "There's a large parcel at the southern side of the lake that is part of the Tinsdale estate. I'm in receipt of generous offer to purchase. Technically it's my decision as trustee but I'd like to know your feelings on that."

"Right now?"

"By Monday at 10 a.m."

"Can I go look at it?"

"I'm sure Samantha can take you."

"Great."

Once we exhausted that topic, an awkward silence stretched between us, which led me to believe that Max didn't want to talk finances with me any more than I wanted to talk finances with him. But I had more than finances on my mind at the moment. "If you have a few minutes, I have a legal situation to discuss with you."

"You haven't been accused of killing someone again, have you?"

"Not officially, but let's just say the new police chief has me on his suspect list."

"Hooo boy." His nose scrunched and his eyes narrowed

to mere slits.

Max specialized in estate law and wasn't well-versed in the subject of bailing murder suspects out of jail. But, to his credit, he'd been a quick learner and had served me well during our one-month association. His family had been taking care of the Tinsdales' legal affairs for more than a hundred years. He worked with me out of a sense of loyalty. I worked with him out of a sense of him being the most familiar with the situation. Not to mention he was the only lawyer in town.

"I'll reheat the coffee," the ever helpful Merry Sue whispered. She disappeared behind the vinyl tablecloth that hung in the doorway between the reception area and the coffee closet.

"I'm innocent," I said to Max.

"Of course you are. Let's go into my office where we can have some privacy. I can't wait to hear this." His voice belied his words. "Hold my calls, please, Merry Sue."

I stepped into the inner sanctum that juxtaposed legal solemnity with Max's wry sense of humor. It was decorated with stately antique furnishings that were what every well-appointed legal office was showing this year, with the glaring exception of the lone piece of artwork, Coolidge's *Dogs Playing Poker*, which covered the entire wall behind his desk. It was not a simple oil painting, but the vivid image painted on a black velvet canvas, the likes of which I'd only ever seen displayed along the streets of Tijuana.

"Have a seat." He motioned to a tufted-leather side chair.

I sat.

He did the same, only his chair, of the same tufted mahogany leather but of the high-back executive variety, was adjusted to full height. Even though he stood a foot shorter than me, the raised chair had him towering over me from across the highly polished oak desk. I felt like a child in the principal's office.

Max tugged a yellow legal pad toward him, drew a gold

Cross pen from his inside suit pocket, made a great show of adjusting the point, then poised to write. "So, who's dead?"

Before I could form Reverend John Thomas Hammersmith's name on my tongue, the doors banged open and in flew the energy force that was Samantha Greene. A recent cartoon run in the Braddocks Beach Bugle had Sam in the role of Little Sprout to my Jolly Green Giant. I stood a hair over six feet. Sam claimed she was five feet three inches, but only when wearing four-inch heels. Her "naturally" blond curls—not one of which dared to fall out of place--framed her pixie-like face. She had the skin of a twenty-year-old and the energy of a sugared-up toddler. I may be ten months older than her, but she looks ten years younger than me. But she spent a small fortune to achieve that look. My appearance was low cost and low maintenance.

Sam always dressed for the occasion. Today her outfit consisted of a black Donna Karan sweater, black, skin-tight Paige Premium Designer jeans and Etienne Aigner black flats. "De rigueur for breaking and entering," she'd said after trying to impress me with the designer prices. *What burglar can afford a four-hundred dollar outfit in the first place?* I'd responded, to her extreme annoyance.

"Did Ellery tell you?" Sam grabbed a chair from along the wall and pulled it into our conversational circle.

"She was just about to." Max's gaze flitted between the two of us in the nervous way of one who is facing two fates--worse and worser.

"We were right outside his office when it happened. One shot through the head. Blood and skull bits splattered all over his desk," Sam declared in a voice suited for the pulpit. "It looked like someone had squirted his chicken salad sandwich with ketchup."

The mere thought of blood invoked one of two responses in me; I either vomited or passed out.

"And the smell. The most gawd awful stench of--"

I wasn't feeling too good. Not good at all. The visual augmented by the aroma was too much for me to ponder. I leaned back in my chair, so far back that the front legs lifted off the floor…

The next thing I knew I was sputtering against a wave of cold water. I was still in my chair, which had tipped over backwards. My legs stuck up in the air as if I were preparing for my annual gynecological exam, and my skirt betrayed me, exposing more of my fleshy thighs than is acceptable in polite society. I moaned, from both physical pain and social mortification.

Sam and Max's faces hovered above me. Max looked worried. Sam looked aggravated.

"Ellery, you've got to stop this passing out when things get gruesome."

"Yeah," I squeaked. The throbbing along the back of my head echoed Sam's reprimand with a clear message that two knocks on the noggin in one day were two too many.

Between the three of us, we managed to get me back in my righted chair. Merry Sue bustled in with enough Motrin to sedate an elephant. I swallowed it all, the day-old coffee chaser being the bitterer of the two medicines.

"Maybe if we leave out the gory details, we can get through the rest of this," Max suggested.

I started to nod, then thought better of sloshing my brains against my skull any more than necessary. With great effort I managed a half smile.

Max propped his feet up on his glossy desk, leaned back in his chair and tucked his hands behind his head, ready for whatever story we had for him. "Ellery, why don't you start from the beginning?"

I beat Sam to the storytelling this time. "From the beginning when Sam had this bright idea to break into the church office during the light of day in order to find out what dark and dirty family secret drove my father from town when he was only eighteen years old? Or from the beginning when we heard the gunshot that killed Reverend John Thomas Hammersmith?"

This time it was Max who tipped backwards in his chair.

Chapter Three

After we were all once again settled in our seats, Max issued a half-hearted request that I begin at the beginning. I started slowly, allowing his dosage of Merry Sue's Motrin to kick in and his emotions a chance to calm down before we got to the icky stuff. I should have been a tad more delicate when divulging the name of the recently departed. I tended to forget in a small town like Braddocks Beach, everyone was intricately connected to everyone else. The pewter-framed 10 x 12 glossy of a teenage Max and Reverend Hammersmith, both smiling proudly with a string of small-mouth bass stretched between them, should have tipped me off to their lifelong friendship.

A glance at Max showed some color returning to his cheeks, so I dove into the heart of the story.

"The only thing I knew about my dad's childhood," I began, "was what Mom told me. On my fifth birthday I asked my dad why I didn't get any birthday presents from my other grandparents, meaning the Tinsdale side. Everyone else in my class had at least two sources of gifts. The few I got came from Memaw and Pop Pop Vogel. It didn't seem fair, and I told him so. Dad stormed out to the garage to work on his motorcycle. Mom explained that something horrible had happened when he was in high school and all of his relatives had died in a tragic accident of some sort and that I should never talk about my other grandparents again. Then she gave me milk and cookies and that was that." A psychologist could probably connect some dots there about how I indulge in cookies to mask emotional pain, and he'd be right on the money. That didn't stop me from eating when under emotional stress, though.

"But the Tinsdales were alive and well here in town," Max said.

"I know that, now." Sam had clued me in on the local legend on how Dad had disappeared the night before his high school graduation. Nobody knew why. Nobody knew where he'd gone. And the worst part (at least in my opinion), nobody had tried to find him.

Max made a get-on-with-it motion. No doubt he knew the local side of the story. I suspected Family Secrets 101 was part of the required curriculum at Braddocks Beach High.

I skipped the part I'd recently learned about my grandmother Gertrude Irene Tinsdale planting my father's obituary in the local paper two years after my dad's disappearance. That way the town--and she--could close that chapter in the annals of local history. On her deathbed a few months ago, she'd confessed to her daughter, my Aunt Izzy, what she'd done. Aunt Izzy had hope that her brother Jack was alive and well, and wasted no time initiating a search. By nightfall she'd contracted a private investigator to find my dad. A few weeks later she'd learned of my parents' horrible fate with a drunken semi-truck driver more than twenty-five years previously. A few weeks after that, she'd learned of my existence, and had hauled Max out of bed at four o'clock in the morning to change her will to bequeath everything to me, her only living heir and last surviving descendant of the founding fathers of Braddocks Beach.

The ironies of life had Aunt Izzy depart this life before she and I could meet. I hadn't even known Braddocks Beach existed, let alone the role my ancestors played in its heritage, until the day I arrived for the reading of her will. One month ago. In this very room. In this very chair.

Having fast-forwarded the story in my mind to the point

of relevance, I cleared my throat, straightened up in my seat and resumed the explanation as to why Sam and I had been in the church at the time of Reverend Hammersmith's murder. "Sam said I owed the citizens of Braddocks Beach the truth about why my dad left town. I didn't think I owed it so much to the historical records, but to my father, to clear his name. He went on to be a highly-decorated Naval Officer and the town should be proud of him.

"According to Sam, my grandmother was in possession of all the family diaries, which is full of Tinsdale secrets, including her own, and going back for almost one-hundred years. Reverend Hammersmith locked them in the church's vault in the basement. My grandmother said they could be opened and become part of the town's history in twenty years. Even though that's still nineteen years away, Sam thinks the secret as to why my father left town is detailed in the diaries, and cooked up this plan..." Max and I turned identical accusatory looks on Sam. "...that we would sneak into the church office and find the key that would unlock the safe that held the combination to the vault--"

"Then we could explore the secret files at our leisure," Sam finished with a flourish. She spread her arms out to her sides, as if expecting us to bow down to her criminal brilliance.

Max and I remained rigidly upright.

"Did you actually accomplish any of these events?" Max asked in his best cross-examiner voice.

"No," Sam and I said in unison.

"Good. No crime committed then. Nothing illegal about two church members walking down the hallway during business hours. What next?"

"As we were sneaking down the hallway toward the Reverend's office, we heard a gunshot."

"I ran to the office," Sam interrupted again. "Ellery ran home."

"Of course I did. You yelled 'RUN!'"

"I meant 'run' to offer assistance, of course."

"What kind of idiot would run *toward* a gunshot?"

Sam dismissed my question with a disappointed look.

I dismissed her disappointed look with a disgusted snort.

"Now, Max," Sam said, sitting up taller in her chair. "Here's what we know. Reverend Hammersmith was murdered—"

"And Chief Bennett thinks I killed him," I interrupted. I felt Sam's eyes boring into me. Ignoring her, I instead kept my eyes trained on Max. He'd shrunk into his too large suit like a turtle pulling into its portable home.

"And why would the chief think that?" Sam's French-tipped fingernail tapped on the desk with a steady beat.

I paused and gave Sam a pointed look. "The chief asked me a few questions that I refused to answer."

"Why?" Max asked.

Tap. Tap. Tap.

"Because he wanted to know the reason Sam and I were in the church. Since we were planning on breaking, entering, stealing and snooping, I thought it better if I took the fifth."

Max's mouth flattened into a thin, tight line. "How did the chief know you were even in the church?"

Tap. Tap. Tap. Tap.

"I told them, of course," Sam said. "It'll be good PR to have Ellery's picture on the front page of the Tri-B again."

Sam was referring to the local rag, the *Braddocks Beach Bugle,* which may look like a dignified small-town paper but was really a print version of TMZ on a local level. When I'd first arrived in town they'd treated me like I was the Miley Cyrus of Braddocks Beach, snapping photos of me at the most unflattering times. I hated that, so had worked hard to stay out of the paper, and told Sam so.

"But," Sam explained to me in that kind of voice one uses on a young child, "you haven't appeared in almost two weeks.

Queen Bees should be front and center every issue as proof of their active involvement in the community. And if we do this right, we can put a positive spin on the way you steamrolled over Buddy Clarke on your way out." Sam paused for a moment then raised her pointer finger and shook it at me as she continued, "I thought it went without saying that Queen Bees do not run people over. In fact, they should always move with grace and poise, at a sedate rate that conveys confidence."

"I'll work on that," I said, eying that finger and contemplating grabbing it and bending it backwards until it hurt. I don't imagine Queen Bees go around breaking fingers either, though

Max must have sensed the tension so brought the subject back to the matter at hand. "Why didn't Chief Lewis interrogate you, too, Sam?"

"Because I ran in to help while Ellery ran away. A sure sign of guilt. Not to mention knocking down Buddy Clarke in the process."

Max sat up straighter in his char. "Was Buddy hurt?"

"Bloody nose," I answered. "And you know how I react to the sight of blood, so I got up and ran to call nine-one-one from St. Mary's. Hey, I ought to get a few points for that."

Sam's finger tapping resumed in earnest.

Max's pen thumped against the legal pad in rhythm with Sam's finger tapping.

My jittery heart joined in three-part harmony.

"I'll contact Buddy." Max offered. "Perhaps we can settle out of court."

"A gift basket is always nice," Sam said with a thin-lipped expression in my direction.

Sam was forever prompting me to send a gift basket, whether it was to offer Get Well Soon wishes anytime someone sneezed, or by way of apology for one of my social faux pas. Since they were part of the Queen Bee role, and technically were food, I figured they'd be covered by Aunt Izzy's estate. I hoped Max thought so too, although we hadn't discussed that yet.

Max stopped tapping to write a note.

Sam continued her solo tap tap tap. "The killer made it look like suicide because the gun was in the Reverend's hand. But he must not have known Reverend Hammersmith very well," she said, more thinking out loud than to be conversational, it seemed.

"How do you figure that?" Max asked.

"The gun was in the reverend's right hand," Sam said knowingly.

Max nodded his understanding.

I voiced my confusion.

"Reverend Hammersmith didn't have the strength in his right hand to pull the trigger," Sam explained to me. "A farm machinery accident when he was growing up damaged some tendons. He could still hold a fork and write with a pencil, but had very little strength for anything else. Especially the hard trigger of an old-fashioned twenty-two caliber Derringer."

"A what?" Max scribbled on his legal pad.

"The gun I saw in the reverend's hand," Sam explained, "was a Derringer. My grandmother had one just like it. We used to play with it when we were kids."

Max didn't seem concerned with this, but I was. "You played with a real gun?"

"It didn't have any bullets in it."

As if that explained everything.

"How was that any different than playing with a toy gun?" Sam's lips spread into a smile that challenged me to argue the point.

Problem is I couldn't. But it somehow just seemed *wrong*. On so many levels.

"It seems we have our work cut out for us," Sam said as she sprung out of her chair. "Come on, El. We need to find the killer before the police do."

"Count me out. Let the new police chief prove his mettle to the town. It seems to be the polite thing to do." Playing the etiquette card always worked on Sam.

Sam grabbed me by the upper arm and hauled me out of my chair. She's much, much, *much* stronger than she looks.

"Come on," she said. "I'm not concerned about the new police chief's image. I'm worried about yours. We spin this to say you spotted the killer and were chasing him out of the church when you ran over Buddy Clarke, who happened to be running in to help. And since you had a glimpse of what the killer looked like, you are in a perfect position to track him down. And when we catch the killer before the police do, all will be forgiven and maybe you can avoid being shunned from society. The way I see it, you don't have a choice."

The way I saw it, I did have a choice. "No," I said in my sternest third-grade teacher's voice. "I swore off tracking down murderers after the last time, when it almost got me killed."

"You're being silly. Think about it. There's no way a person walked into the church in broad daylight without someone seeing him. We'll ask a few questions, because the residents are going to be more willing to talk to us than to Chief Lewis. He's so new people don't trust him yet. This murder is going to be easy to solve, and you will be a hero. Your Aunt Izzy would expect no less from you. See ya later Max." Sam pushed me toward the door. "Come on, El. I'll buy you a piece of pie and we'll discuss the case."

During my brief association with Sam, I learned there are no scarier words in all the land than, "We'll discuss the case." But I never, ever turned down a piece of Reba's homemade apple pie. Not even if my life depended on it, which I had an ominous feeling it might.

Chapter Four

Reba's Pie-ery was a hole-in-the-wall restaurant specializing not only in the best fruit pies this side of the equator, but also serving up the most amazing cinnamon buns to the up-with-the-sun crowd. A bun or two and a cup of their specialty brew coffee was the best way to start a day. Ever.

I loved Reba's not only for its fabulous food offerings, but also for its ambiance. I don't think its decorating scheme was twenty-first century nostalgic so much as mid-twentieth century authentic. Chrome and glass. Black and white. Elvis and Fabian. Poodle skirts and bobby socks optional.

Reba herself, dressed in a white starched waitress uniform complete with stiff, white paper tiara tucked into her tight white curls, approached our table. "Did you hear about Reverend Hammersmith?"

"We're the ones who found the body," Sam announced, in her proud-as-a-peacock voice.

"Get out of town! Hey, everybody," Reba yelled above the din of chatter and clatter that defined the Pie-ery. "Sam and Ellery here are the ones who found The Rev's body."

Next thing I knew, Sam was standing on the table calling for the crowd around her to hush. All eyes stared with rapt attention as Sam gave a dramatic reenactment of her gruesome discovery. I braced myself against the wall and managed to make it through the re-telling without blacking out or tossing my cookies, due primarily to the fact I stuck my fingers in my ears and hummed "Take Me Out to the Ball Game" until Sam was done telling. I knew she was done because a round of applause broke, so loud it was no match for my humming.

I removed my fingers from my ears.

Soon the applause joined in a rhythm, and the crowed began chanting, "Sam and El! Sam and El! Sam and El!"

Sam reached her hand out for me to join her on the table.

What could I do but climb up and bask in the glory of being a small-town celebrity? Especially with Sam pulling and Reba pushing the way they were? It was a struggle, but eventually I was standing above the crowd, looking over a sea of adoring faces. As I've said before, what passes for entertainment in Braddocks Beach never ceases to amaze me.

Sam put a finger to her lips and waited for the crowd to hush before speaking. "We all need to be on guard. There's a cold-blooded killer walking the streets. The Braddocks Beach Police Department has little experience in homicide cases. Now if you jaywalk, they'll be on you like ice cream on Reba's pie."

Laughter rippled through the crowd.

"But they're going to need our help here to catch the killer. All of us. But we can't each track down Chief Lewis to tell him our story, so Ellery and I have been tasked to be the conduits of information from you to the police."

Huh? Since when did I agree to be a *conduit?*

"Somebody had to have seen something," Sam continued. "Any unusual activity today around the church around lunchtime. Or any suspicious people hanging around Reverend Hammersmith. You tell us, and we'll tell the Chief. Together we'll catch the killer and make the streets of Braddocks Beach safe again."

I'd had just about enough of this "we" stuff. I needed to make my non-participation position clear. Right now, before she got me in so deep I couldn't get out. I tapped her with my hip. My intention had been for her to turn and look at me so I could communicate I was removing myself from the killer-tracking leadership team, but sometimes I forget my own strength. Or maybe I just forget my stature. Since my body mass is about two and a half times that of Sam's, my warning hip-flick sent Sam flying off the table in a spectacular in-air cartwheel.

She didn't stick the landing.

I stood back while caring members of the crowd and then the paramedics took care of her. Guilt, sadness, remorse, self-loathing (call it what you will) washed over me as I watched Sam being wheeled out to the waiting ambulance. A double dose of it hit me in the gut when she waved to the adoring crowd.

"Remember, everyone," she called in a strong voice that belied her present state, "if you saw anybody around the church today, or know anything about Reverend Hammersmith that might offer a motive, tell Ellery here, and she'll pass it along."

"The line forms on the left," Reba shouted and shooed people into order. She shoved a pen and food order pad under my nose as the first witness slipped into the booth across from me. Everyone in Braddocks Beach was so quick to help that sometimes it made me nauseous.

Reba also shoved the biggest piece of oven-fresh apple pie under my nose, so all was forgiven. I'm easily swayed by a free slice of anything sweet, but Reba's pie particularly. I multi-tasked savoring the pie, interrogating witnesses and offering grief counseling. It seems our dear reverend was very much loved and respected.

My notes (which I intended to turnover to Sam or the police, whomever I saw first) were as follows:

Helpful Bystander (HB) 1--Claire Burke, a day visitor from Solon, reports an unattended dog running across the church parking lot sometime around noon. Not sure what kind of dog (she's more of a cat person) but it might have had some Lassie in it, only smaller. Suggests owner might have seen something while out searching for the dog.

HB2--Carmen Muniz, a seasonal employee here in town, reports seeing a shifty-eyed man of retirement age poking through the trash behind the church around 11:30. He was wearing a plaid flannel shirt (on an 85 degree day, very suspicious indeed) but doesn't recall any details about what he looked like, just that he had an aura of evil about him.

HB3--Reba Wellington, owner of Reba's Pie-ery, reports overhearing Reverend Hammersmith tell George Greene (Sam's dearly beloved) that he'd recently come into a large sum of money--in the millions--upon the death of a rich, miserly cousin. Her words, "That amount of money is worth killing for. Find out who the reverend's beneficiary is, and I'd bet my secret pie recipe you'll be looking at a murderer."

HB4—Andy Sorenson, the church's landscaper, reports that Scott Carter's green Audi was parked in the grassy area behind the church's outbuilding (he was able to identify the owner on account of the plates…AUDIOS), yet when he (Andy) went into the church to find Scott to ask him to move it so the grass could be cut, Scott wasn't anywhere to be found. "Probably had to go somewhere to wash off the blood so that there wouldn't be any traces in his car," Andy said. Upon further questioning, Andy admitted to being a CSI fanatic.

HB5--Doris and Doodles Rodgers (my across the street neighbors and lifelong residents of Braddocks Beach) reported overhearing some tourists talking about seeing a crazed woman run out of the church. (First thought was "we have our killer" then realized I fit the "crazed woman" description so crossed that lead out).

HB6--Veralee Leinhart, owner of Hansel & Gretel's gifts, reports Reverend Hammersmith had stopped by her store that morning to order a gift basket for an ailing parishioner. His heart seemed troubled (her words, not mine). Suggests that he knew something he shouldn't know and this may have been a motive for someone wanting to silence him. (Upon further questioning she admitted to being a die-hard Sopranos fan.)

HB7--Mystic Sayers, society reporter for the Tri-B, didn't have anything to offer, but promised us $20 for any bits of information I collected before passing it to police.

Needless to say, I ran out of pie before I ran out of Helpful Bystanders, but I tried to do what Sam would have done, if she were here and not off at some hospital getting x-rayed. I felt bad that Sam was suffering because I'd knocked her off the table. But if I were to be honest, the blame lay with her for dragging me into this mess in the first place, so she should be grateful I stuck around as long as I did. Ah, the salve of it's-not-my-fault logic.

As soon as the crowd cleared out, I stuffed my notes in my pocket and my feet in a pair of two sizes too small shoes that Reba had lent me and headed home. As I turned the corner onto Charleston Avenue, my heart did a shuffle step, as it always does when I see Casa de Tinsdale from the end of the street. A statuesque Victorian, my blue and grey conglomerate of towers, turrets, gables and porches stands proudly at the end of the street with Lake Braddock beyond, providing a backdrop worthy of a Thomas Kinkade painting.

While I was standing with my hand against my throat and admiring the view, Henrietta Zucker rushed up to me.

Henrietta Zucker was older than dirt. It says so on her driver's license, or so goes local legend. You'd never guess it to look at her. Through some genetic gift, she had less wrinkles than most fifty-year-olds I know, and beat the white-hair stigma by dying it with whatever flavor of Kool-Aid was on sale at Fazio's Market which today was Roarin' Raspberry Cranberry. To be honest, it's not her color. Not at all.

Henrietta kept spry by walking everywhere she went, which makes that aforementioned driver's license superfluous. The only thing that made me question her mental faculties was the chartreuse jogging outfit accessorized by three inch rainbow-striped platform shoes. I wouldn't make it out the door in those things.

"Ellery. How're ya doing today?" she asked in a strong voice that belied her age.

"Afternoon, Mrs. Zucker. Where's Pipsqueak today?" I'd never seen her without her canine companion, a white yippy terrier who had been my houseguest for a few days and we'd bonded. Well, that might be a stretch. We'd co-habited well enough, but he chose my favorite spot on the sofa as his own. When the time came, he was happy to go home and I was happy to have him gone.

"Today's his spa day," Henrietta said. "Massage, pawdicure, and measuring for his tuxedo. He's going to be the ring bearer for my great-granddaughter's wedding in August. It's her fourth marriage, but she's always eloped to Vegas so she's going with a traditional ceremony this time. Fingers crossed it sticks." She raised both her arms in the air, displaying two hands of double-crossed digits.

I raised my crossed fingers into the air, too. But having more failed marriages than I cared to count in my history, I knew it took more than luck and good wishes to make those things work.

"I heard you and Sam found Reverend Hammersmith's body."

"Sam gets all the credit there."

"Yeah, I suppose. Just so's you know, I don't put much stock in that new police chief. He's a Newbee."

Braddocks Beach had a two-tiered society, not based on wealth, race, or creed, but on where your parents called home when you were born. Those in the top tier were called "Oldbees", or life-long residents of Braddocks Beach (often abbreviated BB, and thus enunciated as "bees.") If you weren't an Old Bee, then you fell into the "Newbee" category which has nothing to do with age, but merely referred to anyone born to parents who hadn't had the good fortune to call Braddocks Beach home at the time of their birth. The oldest Newbee, "No-No" Nanette, is 92-years old. Her parents moved to Braddocks Beach when she was an infant, but she is still considered a Newbee. Although the two tiers mingled socially and got along reasonably well, there existed a distinction, and everyone knew their place. I was the one exception to the rule. By city council decree, I'd been classified a "Queen Bee," on account of my Tinsdale pedigree. The citizens didn't want to hold my dad's running away against me, and couldn't stomach the idea of the Town Matriarch (my Aunt Izzy's title) being a Newbee. I'd prefer non-bee status. Too much pressure as Queen Bee, whose role is to be a societal leader, fashion trendsetter and purveyor of etiquette. A more unlikely candidate they could not have found.

Henrietta was an Oldbee. An old Oldbee. She didn't have much stock in any Newbees, so her comments about the new Chief didn't surprise. I didn't like him either, but I did feel the need to defend him.

"Chief Lewis has plenty of experience in solving murders," I said. "He worked the Chicago beat for years." I didn't really know how much experience he had when it came to solving murders. He could have been a traffic cop for all I knew, but what were the odds of him serving 25 years on the Chicago PD and *not* coming across an untimely death or two?

"My money's on whoever inherits. Money is the root of all evil. Although I suspect the police will consider everyone a suspect until proven innocent. You and Sam will figure it out."

"Sam and I won't be--"

"Oh my, look at the time. Pipsqueak hates it when I'm late."

And with that she galloped off as if she wore Nike trainers, not three-inch platform shoes.

I continued my stroll down Charleston--site of two Revolutionary War battles in 1776 and 1780, I'd recently learned-- and toward my dwelling. Visions of sugar cookies danced in my head as I formulated an action plan that included a cold Coke and something sweet to nibble on while stretched out in the lounge chair nestled under the sprawling oak tree in Aunt Izzy's backyard. Complete, Sam-free solitude.

So much for my fantasy afternoon. By some wicked twist of fate, Sam had beaten me home. Relaxing on a wicker settee, she looked as much a part of the house as the intricate, hand-carved buttresses tucked beneath the eaves. She'd changed into blue linen slacks and a floral-print jacket accessorized with pearls, an outfit more appropriate for an afternoon tea in Savannah, Georgia than for a Braddocks Beach, Ohio, porch sitting. The only thing wrong with the picture was her right ankle, wrapped in an Ace bandage and propped on a white wicker side table.

"What's up?" she asked.

I climbed the five steps to join her. "Not much," I said, not being at all accomplished when it came to disguising the wariness in my voice. "How'd you get back so fast?"

Sam waved a dismissive hand. "I had the ambulance drop me off at home and I called Doc Beatty to come over."

"A doctor in the twenty-first century still makes house calls?"

"A farm vet in the twenty-first century still makes house calls, of course. You don't expect the cows to drive to her office, do you?"

I smiled, not sure if she were joking or serious.

"No time for x-rays and ERs when we have a killer on the loose."

She was serious.

Chapter Five

"Do we have any suspects yet?" Sam asked before I'd even settled my derriere in a gracious, southern-style porch rocker.

"What's this 'we' business? I thought I made myself clear. If I were a cat, I'd be dead because I used up all my lives last time you had me out tracking down killers. I have neither the inclination nor the desire to do it again. That's what police are for. And I made a choice a long time ago to serve humanity by teaching, not policing. But here." I pulled the Helpful Bystander notes from my pocket and handed them to her. "Knock yourself out. Oh, and Henrietta Zucker's money is on the Reverend Hammersmith's beneficiary, whoever that turns out to be."

Sam read through the notes. "The loose dog was Jubilee, a beagle/border collie mix, owned by my Uncle Swifty. He lives over on Saratoga Street. The dog gets loose and wanders back home on a daily basis. Uncle Swifty never goes out looking for her and so wasn't anywhere near the church. That lead's a bust. The car belongs to the Pony League coach who stores his equipment in the church basement. It's a rare day when it's not there. I don't see much else there that points to the killer, but we'll hang onto this for now." She set the notes on the glass and wicker table between us. "You had a phone call while you were out." Sam's voice sounded ill-omened. "I answered it, of course," she said.

Of course. Sam had been Aunt Izzy's neighbor her entire life and felt more at home here than I did.

Silence stretched between us, and I had one of those unsettling feelings that Sam was thinking big thoughts. The kind of thoughts that get me in trouble with the law.

Sam spoke. "Colleen McGruder called to ask you where she should pick up the picture frames."

"Oh noooooooo!" A ball of lead settled into my chest where my heart should be. I was on the verge of disappointing hundreds of children who had been separated from their military mom or dad for nine months. For a four-year-old, that was almost one-fourth of their little lives! I'd promised to make 250 *HOMECOMING 2013* picture frames to be handed out at the USS McDOUGAL's homecoming celebration. They would showcase the pictures that would be snapped as sailors reunited with their families on the pier. McDOUGAL was due home Tuesday at o'dark thirty—that's Navy-speak for first thing in the morning. I had less than 100 hours to whip up the frames and ship them to Virginia.

I had made the promise last May, when I thought I would have the entire summer vacation from teaching, to work on them. But then with Aunt Izzy's death and my unexpected relocation to Braddocks Beach, I had completely forgotten.

There's nothing that made me sadder than letting children down. Not to mention disappointing my Teaching Assistant whose husband was a supply officer on the ship. And now, even if I gave up sleep and eating—which for anyone who knows me knows that's a supreme sacrifice for me-- there just wasn't enough time for me to get them made up and delivered. Sam interrupted my worries. "I feel it my civic duty to do everything in my power to help the police find Reverend Hammersmith's killer."

Save me the "civic duty" baloney, I thought. Sam's only motivation was because asking questions under the auspice of "investigating" played right into her habit of sticking her dainty proboscises into everyone else's business.

"With my ankle the way it is," Sam said, lifting her bandaged ankle in the air and swinging it for me to see her swollen, blue toes sticking out the end, "I need help. And it seems to me, based on what Colleen told me, you need help. It's a win-win situation to me."

"Seems more like lose-lose for me."

"How so?"

"If you don't help me, I'll disappoint a whole lot of military families. If you do help me, then I have to help you and I could very well end up dead myself. After all, last time I helped you play Miss Marple, I came way too close to meeting my maker. Besides, I thought our case, as you like to call it, for the summer was to find out why my father left town so suddenly and never came back."

"Your father left town over fifty years ago. What's a few days' delay in tracking down that information?"

"It's important to me."

"Okay. How's this. I've been saving my silver bullet for over a decade, but I'm willing to shoot it in order to get your family diaries to you. Give me a few days and they'll be in your hands. In the meantime, you help me ask a few questions around town. Somebody had to have seen something. And if nothing else, maybe we can find a motive for the Reverend Hammersmith's senseless death. Deal?"

There had to be a loophole. "We won't have to try to break into the church vaults ourselves again?"

"Nope. Your hands will be clean."

"I won't be expected to do anything illegal, immoral, or put myself in any danger?"

"Not a lick. We'll continue asking questions and funneling all we know to Chief Lewis. As I've said before, the citizens are more likely to talk to friends than they are to strangers. We'll just talk, look and listen."

That's exactly what had gotten me in a whole lot of

trouble last month, but I was willing to sell my soul to the devil in order to not disappoint the USS McDOUGAL's families, and Sam knew it. "You'll help me with the picture frames first?"

"Of course."

"I don't see how it's possible to get two-hundred and fifty of them made and delivered to Virginia Beach in time."

"Everything is possible when teamwork is involved, and that's why Overnight Delivery was invented. I'll make a few phone calls and procure some free labor. We have all night to craft and we can have everything in the mail by tomorrow morning. They'll arrive Monday by ten a.m. Now, are you with me on this?" She held out her fist, waiting for me to tap knuckles with her in a ritual we'd established when we'd first teamed up to find Aunt Izzy's killer.

What choice did I have? I tapped her fist.

"Let's get crackin', then," Sam said. No one had ever accused her of allowing grass to grow beneath her feet. "First stop, She Sells Seashells. I can get us a deal on starfish. We'll paint them red white and blue. We'll hit Big-Mart for paint and glue and shipping supplies. Are you ready to roll?"

"Let me change, first." I felt my black dress and holey pantyhose were too dressy for our crafting plans, so I ran upstairs and changed into holes-in-the-knees jeans and a *Growing Old is Mandatory, Growing Up is Optional* T-shirt.

Within five minutes we were on the road, with me behind the wheel of my beloved Bessie, a dirty and dented Land Rover Freelander. Bessie had been a gift from my third husband about ten years ago. The marriage hadn't made it eight months, but the truck was still going strong.

Sam rode shotgun, which she seemed to think gave her the right to tell me how to drive. "First stop, She Sells. Head up Charleston then take a left on Boston and hit the circle via Ticonderoga."

I didn't tell her I was gonna go that way anyway, in order

to avoid the tourist traffic that clogged the small shopping district on a sunny summer afternoon.

She Sells Seashells was on Tinsdale Circle, three doors down from Tinky's, my favorite greasy diner. "Let's hit Tinky's for a bite to eat. That'll give us a chance to come up with a shopping list."

"You just had pie."

"That was a late breakfast. Now it's time for a late lunch," I said while tapping on Bessie's dashboard clock. Three-forty-seven.

"Okay," Sam agreed, reluctantly.

While I lived to eat, Sam ate to live, which explained why she weighed under one hundred pounds while I tipped the scale at slightly over two. Hundred that is.

As I made a gentle left turn onto Ticonderoga, Sam yanked the steering wheel to the left. "What the--" was all I got out before I heard the sound of twisting metal and cracking plastic. Bessie rocked to a stop.

I sat for a few moments, allowing the adrenaline to recede and my heart to stop skipping every other beat. A few deep breaths. Eyes opened slowly. I repeated my earlier statement, "What the..."

But there wasn't anyone in the truck to answer me. In my rearview mirror, I spotted Sam standing in the middle of the road directing traffic around Bessie and me. At her feet lay a person, crumpled in a motionless heap.

Oh. My. Gawd. I hadn't hit the person, had I? Fear held both my mind and my body hostage. I tried to think back, replaying the past few minutes in my mind, but the sequence went from thinking about Tinky's bacon burger while making a left turn to sitting in the stationary vehicle. No recall of Bessie bumping over anything. Then again, she was a big truck and that looked like a little person. And I had been distracted.

I tried to open my door but realized Bessie was locked in

a way too intimate embrace with a Cadillac Escalade parked at the curb. The two vehicles were stuck hard and fast. And not in a good way. But that was the least of my worries. I needed to get out and see if that heap of a person was okay.

Bessie was not designed for easy access to the passenger door from the driver's side, unless you are a tiny speck of a person, which I'm not, so by the time I made it out of the car, the paramedics had already arrived.

The police kept the looky-loos, including me, away. Sam used her crutches to fight her way through the crowd and joined me at Bessie's side.

"What happened over there?" I asked.

"EMT says it looks like a heart attack. You must not have seen her lying in the road. You were going to run right over her until I grabbed the wheel."

"So I didn't...it's not my...is she okay?"

"No, she's dead."

Chapter Six

We watched the ambulance, sans emergency lights, drive down the road. Then we waited while Titus, the one and only tow-truck operator in Braddocks Beach, hooked Bessie from the back and hauled her onto the flatbed. By this time the Escalade's owner had arrived and we'd swapped insurance particulars. His door was dented but the truck was still drivable. Poor Bessie had not fared as well. Her front driver's side was smashed beyond recognition. My spirit felt as flat as her front tire. She was the only connection I still had to my life in Virginia. I wasn't ready to let her go yet.

"Where should I take her?" Titus asked and smiled. His face glowed with the optimism of youth (Sam said he had celebrated his 24th birthday just last week) and the absence of life's worries. He still carried a wee bit of baby fat around his jowls but beneath that held the promise of strong, manly features. No doubt about it, he'd age gracefully and handsomely. If that thick dark hair held up.

"To your shop, for now," Sam said, making decisions I was incapable of at the moment.

"Will do." He smiled, waved and took off.

"Come on," Sam said, while pulling herself up on her crutches. "Let's eat. I'm kind of hungry after all the events today."

For the first time in my life, I wasn't distracted by the thought of eating. "Any idea who she was?" I asked as we ambled down the sidewalk.

"Don't know. Not a local."

"How old?"

"Late sixties, maybe early seventies. But guess what?"

"What?"

"She was here to see Reverend Hammersmith."

"Did she tell you that?" An unusual deathbed confession, I thought.

"No. She was dead before I got there."

"So how do you know?"

Sam, as always, was two steps ahead of me, figuratively and literally, as she hobbled her way to Tinky's Diner. "Because I found her cell phone on the ground, and while the paramedics were working on her, being the good citizen that I am..."

It took every ounce of willpower for me not to snort. *Good citizen*, my Aunt Fanny. If Sam figured out the woman's identity before the police released the name, she'd get a gazillion gossip points for the week.

"...I called the last number on her recent calls list to notify them of the woman's accident. It went straight to Reverend Hammersmith's voice mail. His private number, no less."

We entered a diner that travel books rate with five greasy spoons. I followed Sam to a back corner table of the cramped and crowded eating establishment. The tantalizing aroma of grilled hamburger and onions, sizzling fries, and strong black coffee distracted me from my troubles.

"Her last phone call was to Reverend Hammersmith," Sam said before I was even settled in the booth. "Ten minutes before he was killed."

"So?"

"So she must have been confirming his whereabouts."

"Sam, you have the most uncanny ability to add two plus two and come up with fifty. There could be a million other reasons why she called him."

"Like what?"

"Like she was a cousin, just happened to be in town and wanted to meet him for lunch."

"I know all the reverend's relatives. She wasn't a cousin."

"Maybe she was tracking down her high school flame in hopes of rekindling that romance?"

"She was the right age, but she had a wedding band on."

"She was probably going to slip it off before she met him. Or maybe she was a hooker for the geriatric set."

"Ellery." Annoyance dripped from Sam's voice. "Show some respect for Reverend Hammersmith. He's not even cold in the ground yet."

"What? Pastors have needs too, you know. And it's no more absurd than your theory."

"You didn't know Reverend Hammersmith the way I knew Reverend Hammersmith. He was as pure as they come."

Good manners prevented me from reminding Sam she'd been wrong about people in the past.

The waitress stopped at our table and I ordered. "A double bacon burger with double cheese, God's way." That was a local term for a burger with mustard, ketchup and pickles, the way God intended it. No reason to lend it the appearance of health food by adding lettuce or tomatoes. "Fries, and a chocolate shake," I added, without a soupçon of guilt. After the day I'd had, I deserved a healthy dose of comfort food.

Sam asked for a garden salad with red wine vinegar, and a half a tuna sandwich. She obviously needed some comfort food, too. I'd never seen her eat anything but lettuce-based entrees.

"So here's my theory," Sam said as soon as the waitress wandered off. "This woman called the reverend, found out he was in his office, then snuck over there and offed him. What a great cover. Who would suspect a little old lady of packing heat?"

"Have you been watching Castle again?" I asked, referring to the show where the fiction writer comes up with crazy solutions to bizarre murder cases.

"Yes, but that's not the point. Think about it. It's the only thing that makes sense. But I suppose you have a better explanation?"

"No, but I'm sure the police do."

Sam leaned across the table and motioned me to meet her half way. "I spoke with Officer Compton while he directed traffic," she whispered. "He said the chief still thinks you know something you're not telling."

"Me?" I said, using my playground voice, not my library voice.

Sam motioned with her hands for me to be quieter.

I complied, to a degree. "Why not you?"

"Because he found me tending to the reverend's body while you ran away."

"I ran to call nine-one-one." My whispered defense fell on deaf ears.

"Do you have your cell phone with you?"

"Yeah."

"Queen Bees don't say 'yeah', they say yes," she corrected me. "I'm going to use this phone," she pulled an ultra-thin, touch-screen cell phone from her pocket and cradled it in her hand, "To call you."

I knew Sam's phone, and that was not it. "You kept the dead lady's phone?" There was that playground voice again.

Sam shushed me with her standard *if you don't lower your voice I'm going to strangle you* look. "I couldn't very well give it to the police after I made a call, could I?"

"Yes, you could have."

"No, I couldn't have because then I would have had to listen to a lecture about obstruction of justice or tampering with evidence or some other trumped up charge." Sam's fingers flew across the touch screen.

My phone buzzed in my pocket.

"Call that number back," Sam whispered while ending the

call from her phone. "With any luck, she'll have a personal message on her voice mail and we can find out who she was."

Sometimes Sam's innate investigative techniques scared the beejezus out of me. "It doesn't seem right."

"What's wrong with making a phone call?"

I didn't have an answer for that. With an audible sigh to emphasize my reluctance, I recalled the number on my MISSED CALLS list and let it ring.

"*You've reached the voice mail of Janet Staunton. I'm unable to take your call right now but if you leave a message I'll get back to you. BEEP.*"

I ended the call and said to Sam, "Her name is Janet Staunton."

Sam opened her mouth and out came a scream that turned my blood to ice.

All the people in the restaurant turned and stared.

I stared the most.

Sam apologized to the crowd and settled back in her seat.

"Who's Janet Staunton?" I asked.

"She's the girl who disappeared from Braddocks Beach the same night your father did."

Chapter Seven

What are the odds that my father's disappearance over fifty years ago had ties to Reverend Hammersmith's murder this morning? Astronomically impossible. Unless it happened in Braddocks Beach, where everyone is intricately entwined. And I don't mean that the way it sounds.

Wait. Maybe I do.

I sat back in my seat as a warm, sickly feeling washed over me. What if dad and Janet had been intricately entwined and I had a half-sibling running around in the world? I didn't really want to know, but I didn't want to NOT know, either, so I asked, "Did Janet happen to give birth that following March?"

"Oh, no. Nothing like that."

"That's good," I said to Sam before sucking down a long sip from my sweet (by northern standards) iced tea. "So what's her story?"

"At first there was some speculation that she and your father had run off. But unlike your father, Janet had been easy to track down. She'd run off with the carnival that had come through, catching a ride with one of the carnies. True love, she'd declared after three nights in the arms of a Ferris wheel operator. Let me think. He went by the nickname Wheely or Wheelsy or something. Janet chucked her college plans and followed him around all summer. Needless to say, that relationship didn't last. I think Wheelsy kicked Janet to the curb down in Cincinnati, but she never came back to town. Not even after her parents died in a sailboat accident on Lake Braddock the following spring. Some think it was a suicide pact. The Staunton's were never the same after Janet ran away. Socially shunned, I'm sorry to say. This was the late fifties and all, way before the sexual revolution, and good girls from good families did not behave like that."

Not coming back for your own parent's funeral? There was more to this story, and I couldn't help but be curious. "Was Wheelsy ever heard from again?"

"Nope. He didn't come through with the carnival the next summer, and honestly, I don't think anyone ever went looking for him. He was not only a nobody, but a no-good, trouble-making nobody." Sam used her knuckle to rub the furrow between her eyebrows. "I sure would have liked to talk to Janet and find out what she was doing back in town after all these years."

"Something else must have kept her away. How does an eighteen-year-old survive out on her own?"

"She was only sixteen at the time. Started kindergarten at age four and skipped a grade."

"Is there anything you don't know about Braddocks Beach residents?"

"I don't think so," she said as if surprised I'd even bothered to ask.

I rolled the recently learned facts around in my mind. "Still seems too much of a coincidence. Do you think Janet's reasons for staying away for the rest of her life had anything to do with my dad leaving town?"

"It was no secret she had a huge crush on Jack Tinsdale. But he thought of her like a pesky little sister."

"Do you think there is any connection between Dad and Janet's disappearances? Maybe that's why she called Reverend Hammersmith?"

"I say it's worth talking to Bing about."

Bing Langstaff was the church secretary. Christened by her parents Cherry Beth and re-christened by her kindergarten classmates Bing Cherry, she dropped the "Cherry" part in high school as a sign of maturity, since she declared double names soooo elementary school.

Everything that goes on at the Braddocks Beach Church of Divine Spiritual Enlightenment is filtered through Bing. If Janet had called the church to make an appointment with Reverend Hammersmith, Bing would get all the necessary--and unnecessary--information in the process. They might have talked not only about Reverend Hammersmith, but also about Wheelsy and Janet's days on the carnival circuit, and maybe, just maybe, about my father. The problem would be extracting said info from Bing. I likened it to extracting a pint of water from a grain of dessert sand.

"Do you still think Janet Staunton killed Reverend Hammersmith?" I asked.

Sam's shoulders slumped. "My gut tells me no. She didn't seem the killing type. But I still think it's unbelievable to me that in a town this size, somebody walked into the church, put a gun against the reverend's head and splattered his brains on the desk, then waltzed out without *some*body seeing them."

I tried not to think about the mental image Sam had just planted in my head.

Our food arrived and we ate in silence. It went a long way toward restoring my can-do spirit.

Since our purses had been towed off with Bessie, we arranged for the meals to be put on my tab. I planned to pay it off before Max caught wind of my frivolous spending habits.

"Frames to make and mysteries to solve. We'll kill two birds with one stone and talk while we drive. Shopping first."

Technically "first" involved me walking home, grabbing my purse that Titus had the kindness of forethought to leave on my hallway table (nobody ever locks doors in Braddocks Beach--it has its benefits, but I'm still adjusting) and squeezing into Sam's Mini-Cooper. I hoped Titus could get Bessie up and running soon. The only form of transportation included in Aunt Izzy's estate was an old beach cruiser bicycle. Suffice it to say its seat was three sizes smaller than my seat.

I headed back to town to pick Sam up, but the delay had us arriving at She Sells Seashells just as Monica Lynn Fisher was closing up shop for the night. Fortunately, she was still inside. Sam knocked and knocked and knocked until Monica Lynn could no longer ignore us

An exotic woman with skin the color of caramel latte and dressed in a flowing caftan the exact shade of orange-cup coral approached the front glass door. She used her finger to point to her wrist where, in a different day and age a watch would be. She mouthed the words, "I'm closed."

"I'm sure you'll open for us." Sam's sing-song voice seemed to penetrate the glass.

"And why is that?" the woman sang back.

"Because I know you underreported your sales on your IRS return last year." Sam returned, aria-like. Sam has an uncanny way of getting people to do what she wants them to, thanks to her knowledge of every skeleton in every closet in Braddocks Beach. There were times I hated it. And times—like now—when it served a purpose.

Monica Lynn opened her door, sold us every last starfish in the house, and gave us a twenty-five percent discount to boot.

It was after 7:30 before we headed out of town.

No rest for the wicked. And Sam didn't need any. She had murder on her mind before we even exited the town limits.

The closest Big-Mart was about 40 miles northwest of Braddocks Beach. I settled in for the drive down the country highway.

"I don't suppose you know the ingredients in veritaserum, do you?" Sam asked.

"Huh?"

"We need some."

"Veritaserum, as in truth serum?"

"Yes."

"It's from Harry Potter. Fictional. Fantasy."

"It does exist. The CIA has some. I read about it in a magazine, but I don't remember what it's called, do you?"

"Not the scientific name, no." I was almost afraid to ask. "And we need it for what?"

"To get Bing to spill the beans about her conversation with Janet Staunton. I wonder how hard it is to make," she wondered aloud.

"Pretty hard, I imagine."

"Yeah." Sam's disjointed response told me she was already five steps ahead in the thinking process. "I think the KGB uses it a lot."

I glanced at her profile, illuminated for a second by the street lights. She seemed too serious for my liking. "Please tell me you have no intention of contacting the KGB to get a dose of the stuff."

"Of course not. That would be silly. I'm just thinking out loud."

"I say we get her good and soused. Hairy Buffalo should do the trick."

"What in the world is a Hairy Buffalo?"

"Grain alcohol and fruit punch. In college we mixed it up in trashcans. It goes down real smooth, and kicks in real fast. And trust me, after a few glugs, there are no secrets." I didn't mention the hangover that lasted three days, or the crazy things one did while under the influence. After all, what happens in college stays in college.

"Bing doesn't drink."

"Not even sacramental wine?" It would take a whole lot more than two glasses, but should garner the same results.

"Nope. The church uses grape juice, anyway."

No more was said on the subject as we turned our attention to the details of executing the picture-frame-making plans. Things like glue guns, craft sticks, paint, brushes and other tools of the crafty people. We added a blow dryer to the list, to help speed the paint and glue drying process. Time was of the essence.

We made it into and out of the Big Mart store before ten p.m. and with less than $500 damage to my available credit. This included packing material and shipping boxes, something Sam had the foresight to add to the list.

We hit the road home. Sam snoozed while I drove. But that's okay with me because it allowed me to munch my way through a bag of pretzel M&Ms without any of Sam's reminders that Queen Bees should not ever eat an entire bag of anything.

It was a few ticks short of eleven p.m. when I steered Sam's Mini-Cooper into my driveway. What I found waiting for me warmed the cockles of my heart. Neighbors come to help us craft.

Doodles and Doris Rodgers, my across the street neighbors, smiled at me as I walked up the steps. I'd always thought they could have been Jim Henson's inspiration for his Muppets. They were round and soft in a way that bordered on cartoon-ish. Tonight they were dressed in matching midnight blue satin robes, and sporting a box of Krispy Kreme donuts, bless their ever-loving souls.

Gloria Stevens sailed in on an aromatic cloud of White Diamonds and a pungent attitude of washed-up Hollywood actress, which she was. I almost didn't recognize her without her post-chemo wig, but did identify the orange and blue box as being from my favorite local bakery.

Susan "Slinky" Davidson (and I'm sure there's a story behind her nickname, but nobody has told me yet) must have rolled out of bed and into yesterday's clothes, because it was too early in the morning to have grass stains on her knees, but not too early for the chocolate-chip pound cake laid on an antique glass plate.

Before I knew it, we had fifteen people crammed into Aunt Izzy's small kitchen, with overflow into the butler's pantry. There was enough food to feed an army, and enough coffee to keep us all awake for a week. This all-for-one-and-one-for-all attitude was one of the endearing qualities about Braddocks Beach. Along with the golden rule of never appearing on a doorstep without food in hand.

We worked hard and fast. We snacked quickly and mindlessly. And we gossiped loudly and shamelessly, to include theories who had killed the reverend, and why.

Long about three-twenty-seven in the morning, there was a knock on the door and Bing Langstaff rushed into the room like her hair was on fire.

"Sorry, I'm late," she said while pouring herself a cup of coffee. "So much work to be done, what with the Reverend's murder today."

We all offered our proper sympathies.

Bing needed to talk, and talk she did, while slurping down coffee and scarfing down glazed donuts.

Come to find out, there was no need for sodium pentothal or grain alcohol. Once Bing Langstaff was coffeed- and sugared-up and punch-drunk from lack of sleep, she sang like a canary.

You could have heard a cake crumb drop when she spilled the news that Janet Staunton had indeed given birth to a bouncing baby boy nine months after she'd left Braddocks Beach.

His name was John Thomas Hammersmith, Junior.

Chapter Eight

"It's called breaking and entering," I said. "And I'm *not* gonna do it."

Sam's Mini Cooper rocked when I slammed the hatch shut. Two-hundred and fifty patriotic starfish picture frames (they looked much nicer than they sounded) had been signed, sealed and delivered to the postman. The overnight expenses brought me to within a few dollars of maxing out my credit card, and less than ten minutes from settling in for a long summer's nap. I'd spent the last fifteen minutes trying to convince Sam I would be much better at tracking a killer after a little siesta, but Sam had a great idea on how to get our investigation off the ground. And once Sam had an idea, there was no stopping her.

Sam's plan to break into Reverend Hammersmith's house in order to find something that would reveal a motive for his murder was beyond whacky. It bordered on criminally insane.

"It's not breaking. I have a key." Sam dangled a brass house key for me to see.

"That you stole from Bing's desk."

"'Stole' is such an unpleasant word. I prefer borrowed. We'll put it back before she knows it's missing. And we're not entering to steal anything. Just looking."

"Yeah, looking through Reverend Hammersmith's private and personal possessions."

"Ellery, you're making this sound like a bad thing, but getting a cold-blooded killer off the streets is a good thing. Besides, we agreed we'd start tracking the killer as soon as we got those picture frames done. I fulfilled my end of the deal. You owe me."

"No. Might I remind you my terms were nothing illegal? Take your suspicions to the police and let them get a search warrant."

"According to my sources, they've already searched and didn't find anything."

"Then what makes you think we'll find something the professionals overlooked?"

"I know Reverend Hammersmith's secret hiding places."

"So tell the police."

"Tell them what? I have a hunch? I'm not going until I have some evidence first. I do, after all, have a reputation to maintain."

I let out a very un-Queen-Bee-like snort. "I'm not going to do it, Sam. I won't risk going to jail. I hate that place."

"We won't go to jail. Unauthorized entry carries a community service penance."

"And you know that from personal experience, maybe?"

"Maybe, but that's neither here or there. We have to do this."

"No, *we* don't." I finger-quoted the "we," which is something I rarely do. In fact, finger quotes are at the top of my pet peeves list, but I needed every tool in my arsenal to make my point.

"Then I'll do it myself." Sam detoured past the parked car and continued down the sidewalk, moving much faster than you'd expect a woman on crutches to be able to move. She turned up the driveway for the second house past the post office and carried herself up the side porch and straight to Reverend Hammersmith's door. She used Bing's key to gain access to the manse, a grand three-storied white-shingled Victorian home, as if she owned the place. I cocked my ear towards town, waiting for the wail of police sirens. Silence. Phew.

I strolled leisurely in that direction, giving consideration to Sam's current theory.

After Bing revealed the reverend's out-of-wedlock baby, the hardworking crafters turned their imaginations loose. Scenarios had been presented, suppositions debated, and the meager bits of evidence examined from every angle and dissenting viewpoints. At one point Doodles and Doris waged a hot-glue-gun war and had to be pulled apart, literally. In the end, the majority concluded the only logical scenario was that Baby Hammersmith had been adopted into an abusive household, and after fifty-seven years of festering hatred, he'd tracked down his biological parents and killed them.

Yes, the theory had merit, except for the part about Janet Staunton's murder. I think that was God's doing. After all, there were no bullet holes through her head. Nor, thankfully, had there been any tire tracks across her back. But we couldn't rule out poison, as Doris had pointed out, without the autopsy report. Still, my money was on death by natural causes.

We didn't have one ounce of evidence to support any of this, hence the necessity, at least in Sam's opinion, of using a key to gain access to the reverend's house to search for something to substantiate the theory. Once she had proof, she'd go to the police--if not of her own free will, then because I'd drag her there myself.

I paced the sidewalk between the manse and the post office like a nervous father waiting in the delivery room. The wind had picked up and it felt like a storm blowing in. Ten minutes stretched to twenty, which stretched to thirty. I started to worry. After forty minutes, I'd convinced myself Sam had tangled with her crutches and fallen down the stairs. She could be lying there with a concussion, or worse, a broken neck. By fifty, I'd painted a scenario that she'd stumbled across the killer conducting a search himself, and she now lay in a pool of her own blood. Why is it that a tired mind is fertile ground for worst-scenario thoughts?

No longer caring if anyone caught us, I stopped in front of the house and peered through each of the first-floor windows. No sign of Sam moving around inside. No sign of a killer, either.

Then I heard it. A loudly whispered, "Ellery."

I looked up and found Sam's face pressed against the screen of a third-story dormer. I rushed to stand below.

"Are you okay?"

"I need your help," she stage whispered.

"Oh my gawd. You've fallen and you can't get up," I yelled back.

"Lower your voice before someone hears you," she whispered. "I'm fine. It's just that I've locked myself in the office."

"How did you lock yourself inside a room?"

"Doorknob's on backwards. Long story. Don't ask."

Before I could ask, the window screen came sailing down and almost bashed me on the head. "Hey, watch it," I said.

"Sorry. Here, catch." Sam threw the house key down to me from above. Come and get me out of here."

"Did you find what you were looking for?"

"No."

That was a relief.

"Don't lock the door behind you this time," she cautioned me.

I felt awkward using a key to gain access to a house without the owner's permission. But the occupant was dead, I reminded myself. And all I was doing was unlocking a door. Saving a trapped person. Worthy of accolade, not a trespassing felony. And besides, Sam had been up there for fifty-eight minutes with no trouble. What's two more?

No sooner had I climbed the stairs leading to the third floor and opened the door than Sam grabbed me and hauled me into the storage/office area. "Don't make a sound," she whispered. "Henrietta Zucker is coming up the driveway."

Worst nightmare--the queen of gossip finding Sam and me going through the recently-departed reverend's most private and personal papers. Definitely not a Queen Bee activity.

"We need to hide." Sam hopped across the floor and slipped behind the beige drape that puddled on the carpet. It swallowed her tiny frame and protected her from being seen. There wasn't enough drapery to hide me. My gaze darted around the room. A sense of panic gurgled in my stomach as I realized this room didn't have a closet. Where to hide? Under the desk? Behind the wing chair? Put a lampshade on my head and hide in plain sight? No, I'd have to make my own hidey-hole. The stack of banker's boxes along the far wall offered the only ray of hope. I quickly moved them around, building myself a nice little fort large enough for me to slip behind. I tucked myself up real tight, giving me a chance, albeit slim, of remaining unseen.

Not a nanosecond later I heard footsteps enter the room. I strained my ears, listening to the sounds of papers being shuffled, desk drawers being opened and shut, a key in a lock, a muffled exclamation of surprise, the chair creaking with weight, then an interminable silence. But to my credit, I didn't periscope my head over to see what was going on. I was not going to risk getting caught.

After what seemed like an hour, the chair squeaked, soft footsteps retreated and silence blanketed the house. I waited for three more minutes, just to be sure.

"Ellery?" Sam called.

I popped my head over the boxes and saw Sam holding an intricately carved wooden box.

"Did you see that?" She shook the box for all it was worth.

"See what?"

"Henrietta Zucker found something in here. It made her squeak when she read it. Trust me. It takes a real shocker to make

Henrietta squeak. And I've only ever heard tales of her squeaking. Never heard it myself. This must be good."

"I thought you already found what you needed."

"I did. I found a sales receipt for the reverend's purchase of a Derringer."

"Which means?"

"Which means it was his gun, not the killer's. Purchased because he needed it for some reason, I'm thinking. I wonder if the police have traced it yet."

"We should tell them, just to be sure."

"Yeah. Okay. Help me get this open, will you? Henrietta found a compartment that had a key."

I approached Sam cautiously, not wanting her to crack the box open over my head, which, judging by the crazed look in her eye, might be a possibility.

Grabbing the block of wood, I turned and set it on the desk. My dad had brought me a similar one from one of his forays into Hong Kong during one of his Western Pacific deployments. Intricately carved pepperwood, identified by the black pepper aroma, depicted a scene of a warrior/dragon battle on the top and sides. With one hand holding the base, I pushed the upper unit away from me, exposing a small block of plain, unvarnished wood. Using my fingernail, I plucked the seam of a crack until a sliver of wood fell into my hand. It had been covering a secret compartment. With a little shake, a small gold key tumbled onto the desk.

"Ellery, remind me to treat you to lunch." Sam pushed me out of the way and set to work unlocking the box.

Inside we found a picture of a late-middle-aged man, fairly current based on the style of the black BMW he leaned against. Behind that was a vintage black and white photo of a newborn baby. A date I deciphered to be February 1959 had been scribbled on the back. A note, folded and yellowed with age, lay between. Sam's hands shook as she opened it. I peered over her shoulder and read the words written in a very precise script.

"*Dear Wheelsy,*

I thought you'd want this picture of our baby. He has your nose, don't you think? As we discussed, I've given him up for adoption. He'll take his new family name of Wannamaker, but will keep the John Thomas, in honor of you. I know in my heart we're doing the right thing. The Wannamakers can give him things we can't. And Johnny will have our love, even if he is never made aware of it. I wish you well as you study for the ministry. My plans are still up in the air. I'm doing well at my job at the diner. Right place, wrong time for us. I will always love you. Janet."

I blinked back the moisture filling my eyes. What a horrible decision to have to make when you're sixteen years old and alone in the world.

"We have to stop Henrietta from spreading this all over town," Sam said. "I don't want to tarnish the Reverend's reputation."

"And just how do you propose we stop Henrietta from talking?"

"I'll figure something out. Let's go."

She didn't need to ask me twice to get out of the place I wasn't supposed to be in to begin with. We turned and faced the closed door.

I'm not sure who was the first to realize we were locked in, but Sam was the first one to cuss.

Chapter Nine

My first thought was to jump out of the window. The chances of the gardenia bushes penetrating my spleen and leading to certain death were high, but that seemed a better option than getting caught in Reverend Hammersmith's third-floor office.

Sam's first thought was to go out the way she came in. She held the doorknob in a death grip and tugged for all she was worth, which wasn't much on one foot. "Help me here, Ellery. You're more substantial than this door."

I elbowed her out of the way. I proved to be more substantial than Sam, but still no match for the seven-foot tall by three-inch thick solid oak door. What I wouldn't give for one of the hollow ones used in 21st century construction.

"Got a screwdriver or any kind of pokey thing?" Sam snuck underneath my arms and peered at the newfangled self-locking knob.

"Nope. I left my pouch of pokey things in the car."

"Ellery, I've told you before that Queen Bees do not make snarky comments." She huffed out a mouthful of air. "Maybe you don't understand the seriousness of our predicament."

"Oh, I understand, all right. I understand I wouldn't be in this *predicament* if you would leave the investigating to the police."

"Well, hindsight is twenty-twenty, isn't it? Now help me think of a way out of here."

"We could set the place on fire, and the firefighters could carry us out on their shoulders. That might be fun."

"Ellery, be serious."

"I am. Hey, here's an idea. Let's call someone." I produced my cell phone from my pocket.

"Who are you going to call? George is out fishing and won't be back for hours, and I don't trust anyone in a 100-mile radius with our little secret. No, the only way out is through the window." Sam crutched herself across the width of the room to the open window facing the backyard, the one that was without a screen from when she'd tossed me the keys earlier. She poked her head out and said, "No ivy to climb down, no garage roof to break the trip into segments, no awning to break your fall."

"*My* fall?" I joined Sam at the window and poked my head out with hers. It was a long way down. A brick patio looked like a great place to enjoy a mint julep on a hot afternoon, but not at all accommodating as a safety net.

"I can't jump. I'm already injured, no thanks to you."

I ignored the stab of guilt. "But the laws of gross tonnage would have less effect on your body than mine. And if I'm laid up with two broken legs and a smashed skull, who's going to do all of your running around? One of us needs to remain ambulatory."

Sam seemed to take this under consideration.

"Morning, Ms. Greene, Ms. Tinsdale."

My head snapped up. We'd been caught by one of the good citizens of Braddocks Beach.

"Why hello, Mr. Clarke." Sam is the only person I've ever had the misfortune to meet who can talk southern without drawing out her vowels. "How nice to see you this fine summer's morn."

"And you. I was hoping I'd find someone on the premises. The building committee meets next week and I need to get the blueprints Reverend Hammersmith was going to leave on the kitchen counter for me."

"The side door's unlocked. Please let yourself in. And

then perhaps you could be so kind as to come up and let Ms. Tinsdale and me out. The wind blew the door shut while we were looking for a pair of the reverend's favorite cufflinks that he asked to be laid to rest in."

"Certainly," he said.

Sam stood there for a minute, smiling down at Buddy Clarke. No sooner had he disappeared from our view then she stepped away from the window and began scrambling through the things on Reverend Hammersmith's desk. "Quick," she ordered. "Find a pair of cufflinks."

Sam attacked the desk drawers like a young child attacks presents Christmas morning. I went straight for his personal treasure chest, the pepperwood box, hitting pay dirt when my fingers wrapped around a set of gold orbs. I secured the box just as the door swung open.

"Mr. Clarke, we are in your debt," Sam drawled.

I looked at our savior, a man of medium build, middle age, and messy hair. The dark under-eye circles gave him a haunted look. About two heartbeats later I recognized him as the man whom I'd knocked over when I'd raced out of the church after I'd heard the gunfire in the church yesterday. It had been his nose I'd broken and bloodied. The one I should have called and apologized to. At the very least, I should have sent a gift basket.

"No, I'm in your debt. I'm leaving town tonight for the weekend, and without those plans I can't work up new budget figures for the committee meeting on Monday."

"You look terrible," I blurted.

Sam and Mr. Clarke looked at me.

I hate it when I speak my thoughts aloud. I blamed it on the fatigue. "Your raccoon eyes look terrible, I mean."

"Ellery." Sam pssped at me.

"I mean, I guess that's from when I ran into you. I'm so sorry about that. I didn't see you."

Mr. Clarke laughed. "Nor I you, or I would have gotten

out of the way."

We all fake laughed, which dragged out the awkwardness even further. Eventually Sam said, "Well, we should be going. Places to go, things to do, people to see and all that." She turned and shut the window, then led our little entourage down the stairs.

Small talk accompanied us, the topic of the Cleveland Indians holding our attention while Sam locked the door and while we retreated down the driveway. We parted company with Mr. Clarke at the post office, with me again offering apologies. He waved them off, then turned and headed towards town.

I didn't breathe again until I'd squeezed myself back into Sam's car. "That was too close for words."

"I think he believed our story. Let me see those cufflinks."

I handed them to her, then slipped the key in the ignition and started the engine.

"This is a sign from above."

"Huh?"

"Buddy arriving before I tossed you out the window, then finding the cufflinks to give credence to our story. I think it's a sign from Reverend Hammersmith that he wants us to find his killer, and he's going to help us."

"I think it's a sign that I've wasted eight of my nine social lives getting involved in your harebrained escapades." I slipped the Mini Cooper into gear and peeled out of the alley.

Sam jabbered on her cell phone and didn't seem to notice my aggressive driving at the expense of her vehicle. "Yes, Titus. I walked by and saw a screen lying in the bushes. Back. Third floor. You're the greatest. Thanks." She snapped the phone shut. "Titus will go by and put the screen back in."

Titus Jones, the tow truck driver who currently had custody of Bessie, pulled weekend duty as the church janitor. His responsibilities included care of the manse. This was not paid work, but volunteer duty. He was a good soul. When it came to role-models, I should be shadowing him, not Sam. "Didn't he ask why it was in the bushes and not the window?"

"No."

"Will he report it to the police?"

"No."

"How well does Titus know you?"

"Pretty well."

"And how much do you pay him to keep your misdeeds a secret?"

"He's on my sweet treat compensation plan."

And I thought all that Wednesday morning baking was for her step-grandson's little league team.

"If you'll just swing by the church, I'll distract Bing while you slip the key back in her desk drawer."

I'd forgotten about that last detail. "Why can't I do the distracting?" It sounded like the safer of the two tasks.

"Do you have any experience with distraction techniques?"

"I have a master's degree in distraction techniques. It's known as a teaching degree in elementary education, but it amounts to the same thing."

Sam sighed. "Okay. You distract, I'll replace."

We traveled the last two blocks in silence.

On a Friday afternoon, there were plenty of parking spots to be found at the church. I pulled into the handicapped one, on account of Sam's temporary disability, and because I was too tired to walk an extra five feet.

"What's your game plan?" Sam asked as she maneuvered her crutches out of the car.

"My plan is to wing it."

"That's not much of a plan."

She was right, but I wasn't going to admit it. I thought of--then quickly discarded--a dozen plans while we made our way towards the church's main entrance. I don't mind telling you, I felt spooked just knowing a murder had been committed right in this very building.

We found Bing on her knees in the colossal sanctuary, a tiny speck adrift in a sea of crimson-red padded pews. Her ash blond waist-length hair was corralled by a black scrunchie which matched her black jacket and black skirt. Her shoulders were shaking as she sobbed and prayed. Lucky for me, Bing was in full mourning mode, and was distracting herself.

Sam motioned her head toward the hallway, indicating that she'd skedaddle along and replace the key. I was to stay behind and divert Bing if it came to that.

It felt intrusive to watch Bing pray, so I slid onto one of the bench seats along the back wall and studied the stained glass windows. Scenes of Jesus tending his various flocks soared forty feet skyward. The detail was amazing and the craftsmanship exquisite. Just last week Reverend Hammersmith had given me a personal tour of the chapel, showing me how generations of Tinsdale money had not only built, but maintained the majestic sanctuary. This was a part of my newly discovered heritage, and I was darned proud of it.

And also part of my heritage was to do everything in my power to maintain peace and prosperity in Braddocks Beach. If that meant helping find Reverend Hammersmith's killer, then so be it. As long as it didn't involve anything illegal or immoral, that is. Or dangerous. I drew the line at dangerous.

At the sound of soft whimpering, I lifted my head and looked at Bing, still alone, still crying. But as I watched, the whimpers turned to wails. Her shoulders shook with gut-wrenching emotion. My heart just about broke in half.

I was not the nurturing sort, but this woman was in desperate need of human contact, and I was the only human around. Not something I'm good at, but something required of a good Queen Bee, so I'd better start learning.

I tiptoed down the aisle and slipped along the pew behind the grief-stricken woman. Gently, I reached my hand out and tapped Bing's shuddering shoulder. She gasped, stood up, jerked around, lost her balance, fell forward and smacked her face against the corner of the wooden pew. Her screams echoed through the sanctuary, bouncing off the rafters and multiplying by hysterical increments.

I peered down at the woman and saw blood flowing freely from her mouth. Her gap-toothed mouth. Two front teeth were missing, and I had the impression her lip had busted open at the seam. I sat down and put my head between my knees before I passed out.

"We need towels," I heard Sam's voice of authority calling out.

"I'll get 'em," a woman's voice called from the back of the vestibule, then I heard the sound of retreating footsteps.

"And bring me a coffee cup or something to put her teeth in. And call Doctor Hill," Sam ordered. "Tell him we're bringing Bing in."

Sam continued issuing orders, and Taffy Allen, the church cleaning woman, obliged. I remained a safe distance away so that I didn't see the blood, but close enough I could hear Bing moaning and sniffling and Sam comforting and calming Bing down.

Sam and Taffy loaded Bing into the passenger side of Sam's car. Sam crawled in the back seat. With Taffy unable to drive a standard transmission, I was prevailed upon to drive the short distance across town to Dr. Hill's office.

Six blocks doesn't seem that far under normal circumstances, but things were far from normal, with Bing holding a bloody towel to her mouth, and a mug of blood-tinged coffee cream containing her missing teeth tucked in the cup holder between our seats. I had to drive six blocks without passing out. I only managed this incredible feat of heroics by pressing my right hand to the side of my face in the manner of a horse with blinders on, which required me to shift with my left hand.

We managed to make it to our destination.

Two nurses wearing scrubs met us in the parking lot and rushed the patient and the mug of missing teeth inside. Maybe if I followed them, the good doctor would prescribe me some drugs to calm my nerves.

"Ellery, I have to hand it to you," Sam said from the back seat. "This is the most brilliant plan ever."

"What plan?"

"The plan to get Bing doped up on pain pills so that she'll spill her secrets when we drive her home."

"Huh?"

"Just one question though. Did you push her? Or did she fall on her own?"

There have been plenty of times throughout my forty-eight years on earth that I've wanted to strangle people, but this time I actually turned around in my seat and did it.

Chapter Ten

"Ellery," Sam gurgled. "Queen Bees do not strangle people."

"Sometimes they do," I growled, tightening my grip around her scrawny little neck. "And the beauty of it is, nobody ever suspects them." I squeezed my hands harder. "How dare you even suggest I hurt Bing on purpose? I would never do that. Ever."

Sam gurgled.

Sanity returned, and I realized that it's not just Queen Bees who shouldn't strangle people. Nobody should. I relaxed my grip and Sam relaxed into her seat and resumed breathing.

I owed Sam an apology. But the words were not forthcoming. I was still mad.

"I'll go check on Bing." Sam crawled out of the back seat and hobbled off towards Dr. Hill's office, looking tired and spent. Well, join the club.

I used my cell phone to place an order from Hansel and Gretel's, my favorite gift shop on Tinsdale Circle. A basket filled with homemade fudge and some locally produced seasoned popcorn would be delivered to Sam's house this afternoon, with a great big *I'm Sorry* card. I placed a duplicate order for Buddy Clarke, aka Mr. Raccoon Eyes, and one for Bing. I asked the $250 bill be put on my tab and sent to Max. I would have to find a source of income before all those bills arrived at my attorney's office.

I settled myself in the car, all windows and doors open to

take advantage of the miniscule breeze, and counted financial black sheep until I fell asleep.

I awoke to Sam pouring a very loopy Bing into the front passenger seat. She giggled like she was being tickled with a feather duster when Sam snapped the seatbelt across her lap. Drugs can be wonderful things.

While Bing acted happy, her mouth appeared anything but. Her lip looked like some horrible collagen experiment gone awry, all swollen and purple. And while her grin was no longer toothless, its sparkling luster had been replaced with the dull sheen of oral cement. To add to her disconcerting appearance, a purple-ish bruise seemed to be forming on her left check, and her mascara streaked in angry slashes down her cheek. The black scrunchie was long gone, allowing her thick hair to puff up wildly and unabashedly. Clumps of dried blood stuck to the tendrils in front. Some caring soul had draped a towel, cowl-like, around her neck, to catch any spare drips of blood or tears. Poor Bing. As my mom used to say, she looked like the Wreck of the Hesperus, although I hadn't truly appreciated that simile until now.

Once all settled in the car, we began our trek towards Bing's house. And Sam took advantage of Bing's medicated state to pump her for information. "Do you have any idea why Janet Staunton was in town after all these years?" I asked.

"Changed will."

"Couldn't she have done that wherever she lived?"

"Left ev'rythin' ta church. Millions. Hadda talk ta Rev. Didn't wanna 'barrass him."

The good dentist had warned us that the pain pills he'd given Bing would make her very sleepy. She started to doze. We needed to get our information before she completely zonked out. The chances of us getting another opportunity like this were slim to none. Although I wouldn't put it past Sam to knock Bing's teeth back out if she thought it was in the best interest of the investigation.

"What millions?" Sam asked. "Janet left town as a sixteen-year-old pregnant girl."

"Taco shops. Twendee-seben 'em. Sold for two point six mil llaaassst..." Bing nodded off. A gentle elbow to her shoulder woke her up. "...year."

"Husband? Kids? Grandkids? Pets? Any other beneficiaries?"

"Nah."

"Sam, didn't you say she had a wedding ring on her finger when she, ah, died?"

"You're right, Ellery, She did. Plain gold band."

"Married in heart ta Rev. Never nobody but 'im."

A mistake at the tender age of sixteen affected the rest of her life. A little counseling might have helped her move on. "Their son?" I asked before she nodded off again.

"Didn't want nuthin from eeder of 'em. Bad blood." That certainly supported our wee-hours-of-the-morning theory our group of fifteen crafters had developed while making the picture frames.

"Killing bad?" Sam's voice rose to a pitch high enough to shatter crystal.

"Bad. Hey. 'Dat's him wight-dere."

"Who? John Thomas Junior?" Now my voice was high-pitched. I surveyed the sea of tourists squeezed along the sidewalks, looking for one who resembled the picture we'd seen in the reverend's pepperwood box.

"That's him! There! Step on it, El." As Sam spoke, I felt her foot pressing on the back of my seat as if that would translate to me pushing harder on the accelerator. I have little doubt were she driving, the speedometer would be toying with triple digits at this point.

"Where?" I asked.

"Turn right. He's wearing a yellow golf shirt and jeans."

I hung a right on Ticonderoga, almost taking a Radio

Flyer full of toddlers with me, and sped down the street. I've never taken suspect pursuit driving lessons. It was harder than it looked in the movies.

The ring of Victorian shops existed within the confines of a perfect grid of north/south east/west streets, with pie-shaped wedges of parking lots squaring the corners. I turned into the northwest lot. My gaze swept the area, then ahead to the tree-lined residential neighborhood beyond. I didn't see any pedestrians, let alone a yellow-golf-shirt-wearing killer. He must have gotten into a car.

Something in my rearview mirror caught my eye. A sleek black BMW slipping out from a parking spot. It looked like the car in the picture in the treasure box. I slammed Sam's car into reverse and we roared backwards. The two vehicles met in a twisting of metal against metal, then stillness and silence. Not exactly what I'd planned, but I had effectively stopped a killer. Now what?

"Get him," Sam ordered from the back seat.

Good idea. I scrambled out of the car and looked up just in time to see the yellow-golf-shirt-wearing man take off running, dodging around the parked cars. Only the guilty run, right?

I took off too, but at a much slower pace. It was obvious that I'd need help, so I started yelling. "Stop that man. Stop him. He's a killer." That was too much information, I guess, because when I yelled the part about the killer, the pedestrians turned and ran screaming into stores and restaurants. I gave brief thought to the repercussions of ending the tourist industry as I did my best to pursue J.T. Junior. That's one of the ten Queen Bee Commandments--Thou shalt not do anything to destroy the tourist trade.

I kept running and yelling, crossing into Tinsdale Park and then out the other side, but the suspect dodged among the slow-moving traffic with the agility of an NFL wide receiver. He was too fast for me, and soon disappeared into the grid of the residential streets. I slowed, and then stopped on the corner of Ticonderoga and Charleston. My hands dropped to my knees, keeping me from collapsing completely to the ground. Inhale. Exhale. Huge breaths to pull some much needed air into my oxygen-starved lungs. I really needed to start an exercise regimen. Or better yet, give up chasing killers.

At the sound of a car horn, I turned my head and looked out under my arm to see Sam's car heading my way. At an alarming speed. I raised my arm enough to indicate the direction I'd last seen Junior, and the car sped on past.

Eventually I took in enough oxygen to get my brain thinking again, which got me to wondering, if Sam couldn't drive on account of her ankle, and Bing couldn't drive on account of she was doped up on happy pills, then who was behind the wheel of the Mini Cooper?

The car sped past again, this time taking a right on Charleston at a speed that had it cornering on two wheels. I jumped out of the way before being flattened into a pancake, but not before seeing the maniac behind the wheel--a tiny, freckle-faced, pig-tailed youth who, if I wasn't mistaken, was Sam's fifteen-year-old step-granddaughter Ann Marie, who had a learner's permit but to my knowledge, hadn't been behind the wheel of any motorized vehicle other than a golf cart.

I waged an internal battle--chase the car or run as fast as I could in the other direction. Away won out and I turned, keeping my eyes on the car as it sped down the road to make sure it didn't come after me.

For the second time in as many days, I collided with another human being. I stumbled backwards and landed in a lilac hedge. As I extracted myself, I heard a car. The Mini Cooper. Heading straight for me. With the wail of police sirens in hot pursuit.

I glanced at the person I'd collided with and realized it was the man with the yellow golf shirt and jeans. The one we thought was J.T. Junior. The man we'd been chasing because we thought he'd killed Reverend Hammersmith. The man who didn't look even a little bit like the one in the picture.

Sam's Mini squealed to a stop three centimeters from my knees. The first police car screeched to within one centimeter of the Mini. The second police car wasn't so lucky, and failed to stop. It slammed into the back of the first police car, which then jumped forward and hit the Mini, which skipped forward until I was kissing its bumper. Literally.

Things got a little crazy after that.

Sam managed to get out of the back of her car before anyone else and held a crutch to the throat of the man she thought was a killer. The cops arrived with guns pointing. They whipped Ann Marie out of the car and frisked her before slapping handcuffs on the shaking teenager. Sam hit the cop with her crutch when he tried to put Ann Marie in the squad car. Sam was frisked and cuffed and joined her step-granddaughter behind the tinted, bullet-proof windows. Assaulting a police officer in Braddocks Beach was not tolerated, no matter the aggressor's social status.

John Thomas Junior tried to sneak away during the confusion, but he appeared to have pulled his groin muscle. At his pace of a turtle on barbiturates, he was going nowhere fast. The cops apprehended him without much effort, charging him with the murder of Reverend John T. Hammersmith, then Mirandized him.

"He didn't do it," I defended him while picking leaves out of my hair. A glance at the flattened bushes had me wince. Cordelia Littleton, proud owner of said lilac hedge, would wage an all-out hissy-fit when she saw the great big gaping hole in her hundred-year-old hedge. Those things take years to grow back.

Officer Compton, the arresting officer, paused and turned to me. "Ms. Greene says she has evidence he did."

"Ms. Greene is mistaken. The guy we were looking for is

about six inches shorter, twenty years older, and has a nose about half the size of that one."

"Then why was he running?"

"I don't know. Ask him."

Compton addressed his prisoner. "Why were you running?"

"Why am I on trial here?" the prisoner asked. "She's the crazy bitch who backed into me."

Compton turned to me. "Is that true?"

"No, he was backing out of a parking place. I had the right of way," I said. "When I got out to exchange information, he took off running."

"Why did Ms. Greene think he was a killer?" Compton asked

This was not the time to protect secrets, so I told Compton what he needed to hear. "Because Bing Langstaff said he was the reverend and Janet Staunton's son, and we suspected he had motive to kill him." We all looked at Bing, snoozing comfortably in the passenger seat of Sam's car, not in any condition to testify. "Bing's on pain pills and probably not the most reliable of witnesses right now."

"What's your name?" Compton asked the man.

"I didn't do anything wrong," the man answered.

"You left the scene of an accident. Let's go." Compton shoved the suspect into the squad car with Sam and Ann Marie then drove away.

That left me, an unconscious Bing, Sam's car with a slightly crumpled bumper, and about fifty people who had rushed to see what all the commotion was about. Like I said, what passes for entertainment in Braddocks Beach never ceases to amaze me.

"Show's over, everyone. Go on back to what you were doing." I recognized many of the curiosity seekers as neighbors, a few tourists as indicated by their paper tour passes clipped to their shirts, and one person to whom I really didn't want to talk to, Mystic Sayers, society beat journalist--a nice term for gossiper--for our local rag, *The Braddocks Beach Bugle*. She had a way of twisting my words and intentions so that I came out looking like the bad guy all the time. But Sam thought her useful, so she'd made me promise to be nice to her.

Mystic stepped in front of me, effectively blocking my path. "Care to make a comment, Ms. Tinsdale?"

The local journalist had paid the ultimate price for years of sun worshipping and cigarette smoking. Her skin looked like a mud treatment that had dried and cracked. She wore a hot-off-the-Discount-Mart-rack cotton camp shirt and capris that didn't look as if they had ever seen an iron. I wished she wouldn't stand so close because her breath indicated she might have hit the local watering hole a wee bit before official happy hour.

"No comment at this time, thank you," I said.

"What happened to Bing?"

"She fell and knocked some teeth out. I'm taking her home."

"Any idea how long Sam will be in jail?"

Hopefully long enough for me to get a good night's sleep. "No. I'm sure Max will do his best to get her out quickly."

"How's the murder investigation coming along?"

"Nothing new to report. We'll let you know as soon as we have something."

"Word on the street is that you were seen sneaking into the manse this afternoon. Care to comment?"

You can't get away with anything in this town. "We had a key and were sent to pick up some things for the funeral. That's all." I'd been hanging around Sam too long, as the lie rolled right off my tongue.

Mystic's phone rang. Her ring tone of the week was Beethoven's Fifth. Da da da dah. Da da da dah. I stuffed myself into Sam's car while Mystic dug the phone out of her pocket. "Sayers. I'm listening. You aren't serious. I'm on it." She forced herself into the backseat of the car. "Let's get moving. The manse is on fire."

The sound of sirens coming from a few blocks north had the local dogs howling. I turned that direction and saw thick, black smoke billowing into the sky. Way too big to be a gaggle of Girl Scouts toasting marshmallows for a s'mores-fest.

The conflagration was more than accidental. There was no doubt in my mind it had been set on purpose. My first, and only, thought was, could somebody be trying to cover up some evidence in the reverend's murder?

Chapter Eleven

Flames shot out between the black shutters that embellished all five of the second story windows of the manse, soot turning the white exterior a grimy black. I pulled my T-shirt over my nose to filter out the pungent smoke. Bing snoozed through all of the commotion, her head resting against the window. I opened the other windows so she could take advantage of the breeze and went in search of Mystic. Sam would have wanted it that way.

I found her in full reporter mode, asking questions of every firefighter, policeman and bystander she could find.

"Any idea how it started?" Mystic asked, but received head-shakes in response. Either they didn't know, or they weren't telling. Mystic had made as many enemies as friends in this small town.

I caught a flash of Kool-Aid red hair out of the corner of my eye, but when I looked across the street there was nothing to be seen. I kept my eye on the stately maple tree that enshrouded a well-tended lawn and sure enough, a full head of Ragin' Raspberry Cranberry curls peeped out before disappearing again. Henrietta Zucker seemed to have more than a casual interest in the events. I dropped my hands to my sides and sidled her way, whistling *Zippity Doo Dah* in a mindless sort of way. "Morning, Mrs. Zucker."

"Oh, my. Ellery, you scared me."
"Shame about the manse, isn't it?"
"Oh, my, yes. A real shame."

Silence. Quite out of character for the chatty Henrietta Zucker. "You wouldn't happen to know how it started, would you?"

For the first time in our brief acquaintance, Henrietta's mouth remained shut. Good and tight.

"I heard you were in there today. Maybe found something of a very personal nature?" I prompted.

Her gaze dropped to the ground as she seemed to be concentrating on the circles her foot traced in the grass.

"I'm not saying you started it."

"I didn't. I didn't start it. I would never do something like that. Never. Ever."

Methinks thou dost protest too much. Given enough time, I felt certain Henrietta would confess. Patience paid off.

"But I was inside when the explosion took place," she said in a manner of a backpedaling politician.

"What explosion?"

"I don't want to talk about it."

"Yes, you do. It's killing you not to talk about it. But I suspect you might look guilty of arson if you do. So what say we make a deal, you tell me about it and I'll get Mystic to take it to the authorities, using her journalistic credentials to protect the identity of her source."

"You'd do that for me?"

I'd do that for me. Since Sam and I were probably the last to be in the house before Henrietta witnessed the explosion, I had as much interest in protecting my visit as she did hers. "Yes."

"Come on."

We walked a half block south and turned left onto Yorktown. The street was deserted. Everyone who had breath in their body was over watching the fire.

"How did you know I was at the manse?"

"Come on, Mrs. Zucker. This is Braddocks Beach. Everyone knows everything."

She accepted this without argument.

"And I know you know about the reverend's illegitimate son."

Her shoulders slumped in the manner of a deflated balloon. "I wish I didn't know about that."

"What were you doing back at the manse this afternoon if you already found out the information this morning?"

She lifted her left hand to her ear lobe. "I lost an earring. Not just any earring, one of the ones I'd made in jewelry class. It won a blue ribbon at the fair, so everyone in town saw it. Whoever found it would know I'd been in the house, or worse, in his private office. That would have looked bad. For me. And for the reverend. So I snuck back in to look for it. I almost choked on the smell of gas. Not natural gas. Gasoline gas. I got out of there just as the second explosion blasted the windows out."

"Second?"

"Yes, there were three, actually. From different parts of the house."

"Did you see anyone suspicious?"

Henrietta shook her raspberry curls. "That's why I hid behind the tree. They say arsonists like to watch their own fires. I was watching the watchers."

"And?"

"Nothing out of the ordinary. I'm afraid I'm not much help. Oh..." Her voice trailed off as she twisted her hands together like a surgeon scrubbing up for an operation. "What if someone saw me coming out?"

"Unless someone saw you sneaking into the house with gas cans in your hands first, you should be okay. After all, what possible motive could you have for torching the manse?"

"If I had thought about it, I might have done it in order to get rid of the evidence about the reverend's illegitimate son. I don't want his memory tarnished. He was a good soul. So he made a mistake when he was young, but who among us hasn't?"

I pursed my lips and nodded. Selective memory allowed me to forget most of my youthful indiscretions. But not all. "Are you sure you don't want to tell the fire chief yourself?"

"I'm sure. I'm afraid the part about John Thomas Junior would come out. I'm not very good at keeping a secret, you know."

I knew.

"You won't mention my name when you talk to Mystic, will you?"

"Cross my heart." Which I did. No benefit would come from revealing my source.

We headed back to the house where firemen sprayed water on the manse from every angle. The surrounding structures had been wetted down, and things seemed to be under control.

I found Mystic and told her I had it on reliable information that the smell of gasoline had filled the house before three explosions. Her eyes lit up. She slipped me a twenty then scurried off. Wow. This investigative business could prove profitable.

I walked the block back to Sam's car. Now, what to do with a snoozing, drooling Bing? I should take her home, but I didn't know where she lived exactly, just one of the many 19th-century homes on Saratoga. Maybe if I drove up and down the street one of the neighbors would recognize her and take over her care and feeding.

For lack of a better plan, that's what I did.

Thank goodness for small towns. A little old man with a handlebar mustache that hung down past his collarbone recognized my passenger.

"Bing lives in the red house with beige gingerbread trim one block north," he told me. "You can't miss it. Carolyn Webster's pulling weeds from Bing's front garden." He glanced at Bing, still snoozing away. "That girl has many wonderful qualities, but a green thumb is not one of them so the neighbors help out when they could. We have a reputation to maintain on this block."

I thanked him and drove off.

I had no problem finding Bing's house. Carolyn Webster pulling weeds was a hard thing to miss. I estimated she tipped the scales at two-hundred-twenty pounds and carried most of that weight on her hips. The local legislatures ought to craft a law that makes it illegal for a woman of that size to wear red and white plaid shorts and then splay her legs and bend over to tug dandelions out of the flower bed. In the front yard, no less.

But one look at Bing passed out in my car and Carolyn raced up the front steps, picked up a pot of decaying marigolds, located a spare house key and unlocked the front door. I carried a semi-conscious Bing, fireman style, to the family room and settled her on a threadbare paisley sofa.

In true no-good-deed-goes-unpunished fashion, Bing's mom would not be off from work for two more hours, and Bing was not in any condition to be left alone. With blood now oozing from the corner of her bandage--okay, I may have bumped it a time or ten when I'd hauled her in--I was not the best candidate for the job. In fact, the sooner I got out of there the better.

With more begging than I've been forced to do since I tried to talk my mom into driving me 182 miles to see The Partridge Family perform at the county fair (that David Cassidy--what a hunk!), I convinced Carolyn's teenage daughter to sit with Bing until Mrs. Langstaff returned home from work. It not only cost me my dignity, but also $25. So much for the $20 I'd earned selling crime-solving tips to Mystic.

I raced out of the house before she could change her mind.

No sooner had I parked Sam's car along the curb between our two houses than my cell phone rang, not some catchy tune that revealed my musical tastes to all within earshot, but a soft, old-fashioned bell jangle. I answered the call.

"Miss Tinsdale? Titus here. Just wanted to let you know the damage to your truck'll prolly run you 'bout three grand, give or take. If you want I can drop the estimate off at your house and you can contact your insurance."

"Thanks, Titus. I appreciate it."

No Bessie for a few weeks, and no money for a rental as I had opted out of that coverage on my insurance in order to save a few bucks, thinking I could rely on my friends in Virginia Beach to drive me when necessary. My friends were now 800 miles away so that plan didn't work out too well. There was always Aunt Izzy's bicycle in the garage, but I hadn't ridden a bike in decades, mostly because large women perched on small bicycle seats do not a pretty picture make.

Arriving at my house at last, I climbed the steps up to the sweeping front porch. Usually doing so made me feel happy. Today I was feeling tired and old and out of sorts. Thoughts of a long summer's nap cheered me up marginally, but before I could get settled in the backyard hammock, my cell phone rang again. "Hello?"

"Miss Tinsdale? Merry Sue, here."

As if I wouldn't have identified her by her breathy voice.

"Max asked me to call you and see if you could come up to the office. Some more bills have come in and he's got some concerns he needs to discuss with you." A brief pause. "He says it's an emergency."

So, we'd moved beyond "concern" to a full blown "emergency." The gift basket bills must have arrived. Every time I needed a little hostess gift (about ten times a week) or needed something to say "Get Well Soon" (maybe twice a month) or "I'm sorry about that, (more times than I care to admit, because I suffer a lot of Queen Bee faux pas), I called Veralee Leinhart over at Hansel and Gretel's and had a gift basket delivered. They were very nice and designed with the recipient in mind. But they didn't come cheap.

"When's convenient?" I asked Merry Sue.

"Right now, if you're not busy. Otherwise he's booked until after three on Monday."

"Now would be fine," I lied. My mom had ingrained in me the Band-Aid philosophy to life's difficult tasks...it's best to rip them off as quickly as possible and suffer only a few moments of pain.

With Bessie in for repair, I was forced to walk the two blocks to Max's office. The weather was perfect for a stroll along tree-lined streets, but only for someone in good physical shape, which I was not. No doubt, it was going to be a long two weeks if this were my only means of getting from point A to point B. What would I do on grocery shopping day? With no job, no cash, and no money tree growing in the backyard, I offered up a quick prayer for some help with my transportation followed by an even quicker "Amen" then applied gentle pressure to the door leading up to Max's office.

The door flew open, practically pulling me off my feet, and out rushed the person I had come to see.

"Any idea why Sam called me from jail?" Max asked, without the societal convention of small talk.

Despite my Queen Bee schooling, I sighed. A great big drawn out sigh. Then spoke. "She let Ann Marie drive her car, but only because we thought we were chasing the reverend's killer. Then she assaulted a police officer with her crutches. But before that we used a key and entered the manse, but I don't think the police are aware of that. Yet. Did you know the manse burned down? I'm pretty sure Sam didn't start it though, because she was in police custody when it happened."

Max raised his eyes heavenward and muttered something about God giving him more burden than should be allowed for one man, and scurried off to take care of business at the police station.

I hauled myself up the narrow stairway to Max's office in

order to set another appointment through Merry Sue.

"Miss Tinsdale, you just missed Max."

"I saw him. What do you think his chances are of springing Sam before dinnertime?" A nap remained my number one priority and if Sam were on the loose, the odds of that becoming a reality were greatly diminished.

"With Sam's reputation, I'm sure they'll let her out on her own recognizance. She's not much of a flight risk."

Darn.

"Is Tuesday convenient?" Merry Sue whispered.

"What time?"

"Noon?"

"I'll be here." That bought me three and a half days to work on my begging techniques. I'd spent a few summers at drama camp, and that may turn out to be money well spent on my parents' behalf. "See you then." I turned to leave.

"Just a sec," Merry Sue said. "Max wanted me to give you the keys to your new car. Your aunt ordered it before she died, and Max says now it's yours."

Aunt Izzy had been a classy lady. The type who would drive a Mercedes or maybe a Lexus. That would be a dream come true. But she had also been sensible, so possibly leaned towards a dependable Volvo. The new XUVs were okay, but not exactly my dream car. Truth be told, I didn't care what it was. The fact I was getting a new car and wouldn't have to hoof it all over town was all that mattered. The power of prayer never ceased to amaze me.

Merry Sue held out a set of keys. Not the kind of keys I'd ever seen before, but I knew technology had made old-fashioned keys practically obsolete.

"The vehicle's out back," she said.

"What vehicle?"

"Your aunt had a car made special order before her death. They delivered it this morning. It's already paid for, and Max says it's part of the estate so you can use it."

My prayers had been answered.

I wrapped my hands around the keys, thanked Merry Sue and skipped down the steps. "Thanks," I muttered to the Big Guy above.

But as I was soon to learn, be careful what you pray for.

Chapter Twelve

The tiny key matched a tiny car, but I only used that word because Merry Sue had. The vehicle waiting for me was nothing more than a golf cart on steroids. A Hot Wheels for grownups. Something you'd see clowns piling out of at the circus. And tennis-ball yellow, to boot. What had Aunt Izzy been thinking?

I marched right back up to Merry Sue and asked her that very question.

Merry Sue looked at me, a puzzled expression on her face. "Don't you like it?"

"It's more suited for a Shriner's parade than a serious mode of transportation."

"Your aunt was very excited about it."

"Maybe as a joke or something. Why didn't she buy a real car? You know, with windows and doors and heat and air conditioning and other modern conveniences?"

"Miss Isabel was very concerned about the environment, and wanted to set an example for the rest of Braddocks Beach." Merry Sue's whispery voice revealed both loyalty to my aunt and displeasure at my reaction to the gift. "She sold her Crown Vic last March and for the last few months of her life she'd walked everywhere. But she needed something to get around in during inclement weather. I saw one in a movie and told her about it and she was excited about the idea. We picked it out together."

I'd hurt Merry Sue's feelings. But seriously, that tiny vehicle was supposed to transport my not-so-tiny body around town? "It doesn't have any windows," I pointed out. "What good is that in the rain?"

"It has plastic that snaps around the edges when needed."

"Snow?" I'm a southern girl, born and bred, and break out in a cold sweat at the mere thought of it. No way could I get myself around town in this open-air conveyance. I shivered at the mere thought of it.

"Oh, Miss Isabel never went out when it snowed. Not after she broke her hip when she slipped on some black ice two years ago. If she had to go anywhere in that kind of weather, Max or Sam gave her door to door service."

I doubted Max would afford me the same courtesy. Another concern popped into my head. "Is this thing even street legal?"

"In town, where the speed limit is under twenty-five."

I wasn't getting any sympathy here, so I thanked Merry Sue and went back down to the vehicle. The only nice thing I could say about it was that it beat walking. But not by much.

I tried never to look a gift horse in the mouth, so armed with the tiny key I returned to the tiny car and headed towards home.

By the time I pulled into the driveway I had a name for my new vehicle. Peep, on account of it bore a striking resemblance, in both color and shape, to the marshmallow chicks I devour by the case over the Easter holiday. I also had a new animosity toward the teenage boys in town who had laughed themselves silly at the sight of me driving the funny-looking vehicle.

Comfort food was in high order, so once Peep was safely ensconced in the garage, I prepared a bowl of fresh-from-the-microwave Kraft macaroni and cheese with chopped up hot dogs (about as gourmet as my culinary skills extend). Thus armed with food, sweet tea and *A Little Bit of Passion*, the romantic comedy I was currently enjoying, I headed to the backyard where I planned to enjoy a few hours of Sam-free solitude. I had just settled into the hammock to eat and read when I heard the irritating noise of Sam hobbling down the driveway.

"Ellery, I've been looking all over for you. I'm glad I found you."

"It's not like I was hiding or anything." The purse of her lips led me to believe she was holding back a comment on Queen Bees and snarky remarks. "Hey, how did you get out of jail so quickly?"

"Max played a Get Out of Jail Free card."

Translated, Sam probably had some dirt on some old Judge and threatened to shake loose a skeleton or two and voilà, she was back on the streets in no time.

"Interesting place, that jail." Sam lowered herself into the lawn chair next to me. Her discarded crutches scraped on the crushed gravel when she dropped them. She then proceeded to give me a play-by-play for the entire time she'd been "incarcerated," (her word, not mine.) As if she were the only person on earth who'd ever done time. I guess she forgot I'd spent a few hours there myself just last month. But I did let her prattle on, focusing more on the cheesy macaroni than what she said. Don't get me wrong, I offered sounds of sympathy where appropriate.

She grabbed my full attention when she said, "You'll never guess who we just helped the police apprehend."

"Obviously not Reverend Hammersmith's killer."

"No, but he turned out to be someone wanted in connection with a hit and run homicide over in Toledo. Isn't that wonderful?"

"Not wonderful for the person he killed, but wonderful for the rest of society now that the menace is off the streets." Thinking of the ironies of life, I spooned one last heaping spoonful of mac and cheese into my mouth and gave serious consideration to licking the bowl. I would have, too, had Sam not been sitting there to tell me *Cats lick their bowls clean. Queen Bees do not.*

"We're heroes. Mystic wants to interview us. It'll be great publicity." Sam turned her attention to her buzzing phone, glanced at the caller ID, then smiled and answered it. "Hello Merry Sue. Did you get the information?"

Sam popped me in the arm and made the universally accepted motion of needing a piece of paper and something to write with. Then she pointed to her wrapped foot, communicating through pantomime that she'd get it herself if she weren't incapacitated.

I sighed, hauled myself out of my hammock and hustled inside to get what she needed. I tossed my dinner bowl in the sink and filled it with water so it could soak. Aunt Izzy's 1950s-era kitchen had not been upgraded with one of those new-fangled automatic dishwashers, one (of many) complaints I had about the old house.

I returned to the backyard, paper and pen in hand, to hear Sam's side of the conversation regarding the Cleveland Indians season. Once I was settled, she said, "Okay, Merry Sue, I've got the paper now if you could give me the details."

Sam repeated everything Merry Sue said as she wrote it down. "John Thomas Wannamaker Operation Smile Abu Dubai will return to United States next Sunday."

Scratch him off the suspect's list.

"Katherine Adair 11062 State Route 5372 East Concord 440-997-1962."

I didn't recognize the name, but predicted a visit to East Concord in my future.

"Thank you Merry Sue. You're a dear. We owe you lunch. Tell Max thanks. We owe him lunch, too." Sam flipped her phone shut. "Time for a road trip. You'll have to drive, on account of it's your fault I can't." She lifted her bandaged leg into the air.

Guilt 101 worked on me. Too well.

Sam gave me ten minutes to change into nicer clothes (i.e. a shirt without food stains) and take care of whatever other business I had. Even though it only took me nine minutes, I found Sam sitting in the passenger seat of her Mini with fingers tapping impatiently on the dashboard.

"I called. Katherine Adair will be expecting us," Sam said when I settled in the driver's seat. "We have an appointment to look at a teacup Persian kitten."

"You're getting a kitten?" I asked. Sam had always struck me as a cat person.

"No. I'm highly allergic."

"Then who?"

"You."

"What?" I slammed on the brakes and the car rocked to a stop right there in the middle of Charleston Street, blocking traffic. "I don't want a cat."

"You're not going to actually *buy* one. We're just looking."

"Why?"

"Because Katherine Adair breeds teacup Persians and is also the lady who sold Reverend Hammersmith the gun that killed him. I needed an excuse to ask a few questions. And once I start sneezing she'll realize I'm not really interested in feline companionship, so you're the interested buyer and I'm just along for the ride."

"Under no circumstances do you agree to buy a kitten on my behalf. I do not want one. Understand?"

I ignored Doodle Rogers' polite tap on his car horn. He was trying to turn into his driveway, but I wasn't moving out of the middle of the street until I had Sam's promise she wasn't going to make me buy a cat. Not even if it came with the name, address and social security number of Reverend Hammersmith's killer.

"Cats are wonderful companions."

"No cats."

"That house is too big for you to live in alone."

"No cats."

Honk. Honk.

"The mice will invade when the weather changes."

"That's why mousetraps were invented. I do not want a cat. Are we clear?"

"Perfectly." Sam didn't sound the least defeated. "We'll say it's a birthday present for my granddaughter."

I offered an apologetic finger wave to Doodles, then put the Mini Cooper in gear and we eased on down the road.

Thirty minutes later we spotted a small gray sign that advertised *Kat's Cattery. Teacup Persians. Visitors Welcome.* Two minutes after that we pulled up to a cozy cabin in the woods. Katherine Adair met us on the front porch. She was a tall, heavyset woman with a face as flat as the Persians she bred. I'd put her in the sixty-something category in age, on account of the shapeless floral housedress she was wearing reminded me of my own Granny Vogel at that age.

"You must be Miss Tinsdale and Miss Greene," she said, her voice low and raspy. "Please come in."

We stepped inside, and I time-warped back to my maternal grandmother's living room. Tweed sofas, shag carpet and piles of glossy Hollywood magazines transported me back to the 60s. I breathed deeply, expecting to fill my head with the smell of Granny Vogel's Channel Number Five perfume, but instead choked against the stench of tomcat territory markings. That's another reason I don't like cats.

Sam sneezed.

Katharine Adair handed Sam a box of tissues. "I'm sorry, I'm not as much of a housekeeper as I used to be."

Judging by the dust on the TV set, she hadn't been much of a housekeeper since the turn of the century.

"So you're here to see Sinatra? Great lineage. Midnight Mist out of Starship Enterprise. Last of the litter. He's a bit on the puny side, but cuddly as they come." Katharine splayed her feet and bent from the waist (her housedress riding high to reveal knee-high stockings) to extract a tiny bundle of misty-colored fur from beneath the gold sofa.

Electric blue eyes peered from his perch on Katherine's shoulder. I'm not sure, but I think he smiled at me.

Kat handed me the kitten, which snuggled under my chin and purred loudly. My heart melted.

"Let's sit down."

We did, and I snuggled with the silky bundle of thrumming energy while Sam and Kat conversed. Well, Sam talked between sneezes. I wasn't listening. I put Sinatra on the sofa next to me and tapped my fingers toward him, then retreated. I moved my fingers forward, he shrunk back, then pounced when my hand pulled back. We played for a few minutes, then Sinatra crawled onto my lap. I stroked his silky fur while he purred like a Mac truck. Maybe a cat would be good company.

Pain. So sharp it took my breath away.

I extracted Sinatra's fangs from my thumb and watched two small dots of blood appear. That erased the tenuous bond we had formed. No cats for me.

I put the kitten on the ground and turned my attention to the conversation that seemed to be taking a significant turn.

"I heard about you through Reverend Hammersmith. We're from Braddocks Beach," Sam said. "He's our pastor. Or was."

"Oh, dear," Katherine said. "Did something happen?"

"You didn't hear?"

Katherine shook her head.

"He was killed yesterday. Shot dead as he sat in his chair preparing Sunday's sermon."

Katherine's face turned the color of cream of mushroom soup. "Shot?"

"With an old-fashioned pearl-handled Derringer."

Katherine slouched back against a red and black granny-square afghan. "A derringer?"

Sam nodded.

"Pearl-handled you say?"

Sam nodded again.

"I sold him my grandfather's old derringer just last week." Her voice was barely more than a whisper, and I wasn't sure if she was talking to us or herself.

"You sold the reverend a gun?" Sam asked with such genuine surprise I considered nominating her for an Emmy.

"Yes. I was going through some old boxes in the attic, looking for something interesting to take to Antiques Roadshow when it rolls through Columbus at the end of the month. The gun wasn't worth much, according to a Google search, so I put an ad in the paper. Reverend Hammersmith called me and came out a week ago today. He said he needed it for show, not to use."

Sam inched forward to the edge of her seat. "For show? As in a gun show or something?"

"No. He said somebody was threatening him and he thought if things got sticky he'd flash the gun. He didn't care if it worked or not. Seemed to think that was all it would take to scare this person off."

That confirmed what Veralee Leinhart had told us about the reverend's heart seeming troubled when he'd stopped in to order a gift basket.

I inched forward to the edge of my seat. "Did he give any hint who? He? She? Or why?"

Katherine seemed to be pushing away the cobwebs of recent conversations, then slowly shook her head. "No, he tried to play it down, but he practically jumped at his own shadow. I remember thinking that now."

Despite a long, unsettling silence, Katherine Adair didn't come up with any more information that might help us figure out who had put the fear of God in our dear reverend.

Chapter Thirteen

"We need to talk to Bing," Sam said as we headed back into town after she put a deposit down on Sinatra. "Maybe she knew who was bothering the Rev."

"What could Bing possibly know about the Adair-Hammersmith connection?" I asked.

"Nothing, but I'm hoping she'll know who was scaring the beejezus out of Reverend Hammersmith."

According to the dashboard clock it was 9:38. Eight minutes past my bedtime. More like twenty-four hours and eight minutes past bedtime, considering we never had gone to sleep last night.

"Let's drive by her house and see if she's still up."

As many pain meds as Bing had taken, my guess was she'd been asleep for hours. But since her house wasn't too far out of our way, I figured it was easier to appease Sam than try to argue her out of the idea.

We drove in silence through the quiet streets. Turning onto Saratoga Street, it looked as if the entire neighborhood was tucked in for the night. I slowed in front of Bing's house.

"Look. Her bedroom light's on," Sam said.

I peered up to the darkened house. There was a weak glow in an upstairs window, but it looked more like a nightlight than an I'm-up-and-ready-to-receive-visitor's light. But try telling that to Sam. She was out of the car and hobbling up the sidewalk before I had the engine turned off.

I joined Sam at the front door, where I found her laying

on the doorbell like a New York taxi driver lays on a horn in a traffic jam. After three long doorbell presses and numerous loud knocks, a sleepy-headed Bing answered. She seemed surprised to see us. Maybe surprised was a stretch. Irritated might be a more accurate description.

"Aren't you going to invite us in?" Sam asked. But the question was rather redundant, as Sam had already placed the rubber nubs of her crutches on the entryway's highly polished parquet floor and her body was swinging forward. "Let's go into the parlor."

"Where are my manners?" Bing asked, but in a tone belying her concern for social niceties. "Let me ring for a butler to bring some tea and scones."

"No cause to be snappish, Bing," Sam said.

I felt there was plenty of cause to be snappish. If someone had come to my house after I went to bed, I wouldn't even answer the door.

"This is not a social call. This is business." Sam disappeared into another room.

Bing followed. I brought up the rear as we filed into the front parlor. Only in Braddocks Beach will you still find parlors. They'd been all the rage in Victorian times. The cozy quarters made them perfect for sitting around and sipping tea, pinky finger properly extended, while sharing secrets. Other people's secrets, that is. Never their own.

While the rest of the country had since converted the tiny front rooms into home offices or playrooms for toddlers, most parlors in Braddocks Beach maintained their original purpose, Bing's included. Decorated straight out of *Victorian Secrets* magazine, the focal points were the matching table lamps with fringed shades set on antique-looking tables with simple yet elegant lines. The tables flanked a camelback sofa. Side chairs covered in heavy brocade the color of Merlot sat opposite the sofa. Lots of porcelain figurines and interesting glassware filled the built-in shelves in the corner. The furnishings could be authentically Victorian or Bob's Discount Warehouse knock-offs. I'm not an expert on antiques. I'm not even a novice.

I settled onto the sofa while Sam perched on a side chair. Bing took a seat on another side chair, propped her elbow on the armrest and plopped her chin in her cupped hand.

"What kind official business couldn't wait until Monday morning?" Bing asked, her eyes at half-mast, her lip at full, swollen attention.

It hurt me just to look at it.

"The official business of solving Reverend Hammersmith's murder," I said, sensing Sam was about to follow the rules of polite conversation by leading in with six minutes, and I mean to the last 360th second, of banal chatter before getting to the purpose of our visit. The quicker we finished our business, the sooner Bing could go back to bed. Me, too.

"We've recently been told the good reverend was so afraid of someone that he'd purchased a gun," Sam said.

Bing sat up in her chair and gave a tug on the belt of her yellow chenille bathrobe.

"We know you know who that is, and we suspect very strongly that's who killed him."

Bing shifted in her seat in the unconscious mannerism of someone who was about to tell a whopper. "I don't know what you're talking about," she said in a strong voice that contradicted her body language.

"Yes, you do," I said. "Someone was threatening him. He was so frightened he purchased a gun, the very same gun which was used to kill him."

Silence.

"Who was it?" I asked again.

Silence.

"Did he tell you?" Sam asked.

Silence.

"Did you figure it out yourself?" I asked, giving her a way to keep the reverend's confidences, if that's what she was worried about.

Silence.

This was getting tedious.

Sam got out of her chair and maneuvered herself until she was standing next to one of the end tables. She oh-so-casually reached out and picked up a vase, a flowery number, made of delicate porcelain. Possibly ancient Chinese, but again, I'm no expert.

Bing gasped and jumped out of her chair. "Don't touch that," she shouted. "It was a gift to my great grandmother from the Queen Mother…" Bing's voice trailed off.

"I won't break it," Sam assured her while tossing the vase from one hand to another as if it were a hot potato. "Not if you tell us what you know." Sam tossed the vase a few inches into the air then caught it and pulled it in under her arm like a wide receiver tucks in a football. Then she leveled a most accusing stare at Bing.

Bing started pacing the length of the small parlor. As she did so, she buffed her nails against her bathrobe in a frantic back and forth motion. Her head started twisting from side to side, as if she were working out a kink. Then she stopped right in the middle of the room. She stood so still, I think she may have even stopped breathing.

Sam tossed the vase again.

Bing started speaking. "You're right, someone had threatened Reverend Hammersmith." She took a deep breath, and despite the fact that neither Sam nor I are ordained, she gave a full confessional.

"I had a lover." Her words were barely a whisper. I had to lean towards her in order not to miss a word. "Only he was married to another woman. The reverend found out about it and was counseling us to end it, only we didn't want to, and my lover didn't want to leave his wife on account of some financial issues, but he didn't love her, he loved me, and we were going to work things out eventually, but the reverend had said something to my lover's wife and it all threatened to be exposed, and you know what would happen if the grapevine got wind of that. We'd all be banished from Braddocks Beach."

I observed a moment of silence to digest the words. There were a lot of "love" references that had things a bit tangled, but I think I got the picture. "So," I said, rather fearful of what I was about to say, but it had to be said. "Were you the one threatening Reverend Hammersmith?"

"No!" Bing answered with great conviction.

I believed her.

"Your lover threatened the reverend?" I asked, slapping the heel of my hand against my temple as I connected the dots. He would be the obvious one.

"No, he wanted to do what the reverend suggested and come clean."

"I bet he snapped," I said, settling back in my seat. "I bet it was all a front to make him seem not the killing type, but I bet he snapped."

"No, I know it wasn't him," Bing said.

"How can you be sure?" Sam asked.

"I can provide his alibi." Bing's gaze darted between Sam and me. "We were together at the time of the reverend's death."

"Where?" I asked.

"At the church. In the green room. On the couch. Being, ah, intimate." Bing slapped her hand to her injured lip as if to push the secret she'd just revealed back into her mouth, then winced in pain.

I, too, wish she hadn't shared her secret. That fell into the TMI category...too much information. Way too much.

"If not either of you, then who?" Sam asked as she raised the vase above her head.

"It was my lover's wife," Bing revealed. "She wanted Reverend Hammersmith to butt out. Said she'd handle things her way, and threatened him if he said so much as one word. She had him spooked, all right. And I wouldn't be surprised if she'd killed him."

"I need a name, Bing." Sam said. "Who was your lover? I'll tell the police and keep your name out of it, I promise. But if his wife was threatening Reverend Hammersmith, she had motive for murdering him, too."

Bing paused, using her index figure to rub the furrow between her brows, a sure sign of a headache in the making.

Sam wiggled the vase above her head.

Bing held up her hand to stop Sam from tossing the vase, which obviously had great sentimental--if not monetary--value, then whispered the name we'd been waiting to hear. "Scott Carter."

That name meant nothing to me, but it had an effect on Sam. The poor woman looked like she was going to faint. She made a weak attempt to fall back onto the chair, and in the process the vase slipped from her hands and smashed against the wood floor, shattering into a ba-zillion shards of porcelain.

Bing lunged across the room and tackled Sam to the ground. The two rolled and thrashed around in a match that was straight out of a Girls Gone Wild episode, only with the slightly older wrestlers. And with less flesh showing.

They rolled around on the wood floor, knocking into tables and chairs. By some miracle, no other fragile items broke.

Sam's hands were wrapped around Bing's neck. Bing's hands were wrapped around Sam's neck. Both of their faces were an unnatural shade of red that reminded me of Campbell's Tomato Soup.

Braddocks Beach was going to lose another citizen if I didn't do something to put an end to this nonsense.

Chapter Fourteen

I managed to pull Sam and Bing apart and get Sam out of the house without any of the three of us suffering serious injury.

"What was that all about?" I asked when we were tucked in the Mini and heading home.

"I don't want to talk about it."

"Who is Scott Carter?"

"I don't want to talk about it."

"And why would his wife kill Reverend Hammersmith and not Scott? Or Bing?"

"I said I don't want to talk about it."

"Fine. We'll phone in an anonymous tip to the police then tumble into our respective beds for a much deserved night of sleep." I fished my cell phone out of my pocket and handed it to her. "With any luck, they'll have the killer locked up by the time we're eating breakfast tomorrow."

Sam looked at the phone for a few minutes, then dropped it into the cup holder between us. "Scott Carter is Brian's best friend," she revealed.

"Your stepson Brian?" Brian was one year older than Sam, but she still thought of Brian like a son.

"Yes. Friends since their diaper days."

She might have known him herself in school. Small towns are funny that way. "Still friends?"

"Yes. Scott is RJ's baseball coach."

RJ was Sam's step-grandson, a ten-year-old toe-headed

child who was blessed with equal parts charm and mischief. Sam doted on the boy.

"You met him at the game last week. Melissa, his wife, was there, too. I pointed her out to you."

I remembered Scott, a tall, natural athlete with sandy blond hair. I don't think I'd ever heard his name, as everyone referred to him as "Coach," even the parents. If memory served, Scott's career was that of a professional volunteer. It was his wife's money that enabled him to not work and focus his energy on running the local pony league. He coached, too, and my impression had been he was good at it. He encouraged the boys, didn't yell at them when they missed the ball or made a bad play, and taught them to think one play ahead. He seemed like a good guy. Not a killer. And not a philanderer, either.

"So you think Bing is lying?" I maneuvered our car under the large maple tree in her driveway and cut the engine and dimmed the lights. I didn't make a move to get out, on account of I thought that would end the conversation, and Sam needed to talk right now. So I'd listen. For a bit, anyway.

Sam slumped in her seat. "Didn't you say Andy Sorenson saw Scott's Audi behind the church at the time the reverend was killed?"

I thought back to my Helpful Bystander notes. While I didn't remember the names, I did remember the catchy license plate. "Audios?"

Sam nodded. "So Scott was at the church, but Andy didn't find him in the basement, meaning Scott was somewhere else in the church. That supports Bing's confession they were together in the green room."

"But were they together in killing Reverend Hammersmith?"

Sam gave her dashboard the white glove test then stared at the dust on her finger before wiping it on her pants. "If Bing felt the need to lie her way into an alibi, I can't see how saying she was engaged in extracurricular activities with another woman's husband is the best cover. I have to think she was telling the truth." Sam took another swipe at the dashboard. "I'm just having a hard time accepting it, that's all."

"Did Scott and Melissa have a loving marriage?"

"I don't know. They got married quickly, for the usual reasons."

"Madly in love?"

"Hardly. She had a bun in the oven."

"Did she have the baby?"

Sam shook her head. "Miscarriage. Seventeenth week."

I don't know what Sam was thinking, but my mind wondered if there'd ever been a baby to begin with, or had Melissa employed the oldest trick in the book. "I don't get what all the fuss was about divorcing her, then," I said.

"Standard pre-nup. It's her family money. Scott doesn't stand to get a single cent if he files for divorce. She has to do it."

"So if Melissa knew about Scott's affair with Bing, why didn't she file for divorce and then she'd get to keep her money?"

Sam chewed on her lower lip for a few minutes before answering. "She obviously didn't want a divorce, or she wouldn't have threatened Reverend Hammersmith to stay out of it."

"There's more to that story, I'm sure." I was also sure it was bugging Sam beyond all get out that an affair of the flesh had been happening right under her nose, and she hadn't caught wind of it.

I thought about Scott's wife Melissa who had been pointed out to me at the ball field. A tall woman who would stand out in any crowd, she was doubly notable the night I'd seen her on account of her outfit. Despite a damp, misty twilight game where most people sported jeans and sweatshirts, Melissa had worn a designer sun dress, flashy stiletto shoes, and a huge floppy hat that had reminded me of Julia Roberts and her polo match scene in *Pretty Woman*. Melissa hadn't exactly been playing the role of doting wife during the game, and if memory served had scowled the entire time, when she wasn't tapping the screen on her blackberry or filing her nails. It could be she'd been miffed that Mother Nature hadn't provided her with the perfect summer weather to accessorize her outfit, or it could have been that her husband's lover was sitting in the stands with Sam and me three rows behind her. Now that I think about it, her countenance could have been that of one plotting murder, although Melissa didn't appear to be the type who would risk getting blood on her hands and brain splattered on her clothes, which is the collateral damage when holding a gun to someone's head and pulling the trigger. Nope, these puzzle pieces weren't fitting at all.

"Do you think Melissa killed Reverend Hammersmith as Bing suggested?" I asked Sam.

"I can see her not wanting Scott's affair broadcast, no woman does, but I can't see it being worth killing for. I say we talk to Scott's mom." Sam fished her cell phone out of her pocket and scrolled through her list of contacts.

"Not tonight," I said, aghast at the thought. Even before I'd become a Queen Bee I knew it wasn't polite to call anyone after ten p.m. And it was half-past ten now.

"Yes, tonight. I can't in good conscience set the police on Melissa without all the facts." Sam put her phone to her ear. "Hello, Irene? Sam Greene here. Yes, lovely weather. Rain next week, I hear. Listen, it's late and I want to keep this quick. I'm helping Chief Lewis with the investigation of Reverend Hammersmith's murder, and it has come to our attention that Melissa may have had motive and opportunity to kill him. I need to know why she didn't want to divorce Scott, even though she knew of his peccadilloes, and where Melissa was last Thursday around noon." Sam listened, uh-huh'd a lot, then rang off.

"Okay," she said to me. "Simple case of sibling rivalry. When Melissa's sister Rhonda divorced her husband for his wandering ways a few years back, Melissa made quite a fuss about how Rhonda couldn't hold on to her man, and never ever let her forget it. Knowing Melissa, that had to have been brutal. So it's a matter of pride and fear of having her words thrown back in her face that Melissa wants to keep her marriage intact. No motive for murder there. And I confirmed Melissa was volunteering at the Blood Bank from 10 a.m. to 4 p.m. on Thursday. She didn't even take a lunch break. So without motive or opportunity, she's not our killer."

Sam opened the door to the car but paused before getting out. "Did you send a gift basket to Bing today?" Sam asked.

"Yup. With a nice big 'Hope your mouth feels better soon' card." I was slowly getting the hang of this Queen Bee thing.

"You might want to send another one. You know, on account of the vase and all."

Far be it from me to point out that Sam had been the one to drop the vase, not me. Now would be a good time to share with her the facts of my financial life, in that I was poorer than the proverbial church mouse, not the richest woman in all of Braddocks Beach who could go around covering her expenses. But I wasn't quite ready to divulge the terms of Aunt Izzy's will. Not yet.

I made a mental sticky note to call Hansel and Gretel's tomorrow to take care of that.

"If you wait here, I'll bring you a few éclairs left over from Wednesday's bridge tournament. I'd invite you in, but I imagine George is snoozing in front of the news again, and I can't guarantee he's dressed."

"No problem. I'll wait." I settled back in the seat, once again feeling confined in the small space, and waited for Sam to bring the éclairs out.

The next thing I knew the sun's morning rays were prying my eyelids open. I sat up, wiped the drool from my chin, rubbed at the puddle on my shirt and tried to work the crick out of my neck. Then I spotted the bakery box of éclairs on the seat next to me. What a fabulous way to start a new day!

I unfurled myself from the tight confines of Sam's car and stretched toward the cloudless blue sky. When I tried to touch my toes, a bolt of pain shot from my lower back to the base of my skull. Okay, enough exercise for today.

I grabbed the bakery box and headed towards the break in the hedge between Sam's house and mine. The sound of men's voices stopped me in my tracks. Not so much the sound itself, but the tone, coming from Sam's opened kitchen window. Very hush hush. Which meant I wasn't supposed to hear. But when I heard Bing's name, I felt a proprietary interest (since I knew her deepest darkest secrets and all). Without conscious thought, I positioned myself underneath the Greene's opened kitchen window and listened.

"Bing took an overdose of pain pills last night."

My hand flew to my mouth, stifling the gasp. Her attempted suicide was undoubtedly a result of us forcing her to confess her sins to us last night. And we weren't even ordained. My heart ached for Bing.

"Is she dead?" That was George. He was a shoot-from-the-hip kind of guy.

"No, she's gonna be okay. She's in the psych ward for observation. It's all my fault."

I didn't recognize the voice of the man speaking, but felt relief at this bit of news. A super-sized gift basket would be on its way as soon as Hansel and Gretel's opened this morning.

"You can't hold yourself responsible for other people's actions."

I peeked through the window but couldn't see anyone. They must be around the corner in the breakfast nook. I pressed my ear to the screen, knowing full well that eavesdropping was wicked, but I needed to know who George was talking to and something inside me said I wouldn't find out this information any other way.

"I know," the stranger's voice resumed talking. "But if I'd ended our relationship like you told me to, none of this would have happened. If our secret gets out, well, lives will be ruined."

Ah, the person speaking must be Scott Carter. Am I a brilliant detective or what?

"There's no happy ending here." George was speaking.

"What am I going to do?" I heard the unmistakable sound of a glass smashing against the tile floor. The force led me to conclude it had been thrown, not dropped.

I would have really, really wanted to hear the answer to this question, but the sound of a yippy dog gave me warning that Mrs. Weatherby and her pampered pooch were enjoying their early morning constitutional. Standing here with my ear to the screen, I was sure to get caught eavesdropping. And if there's one rule I've committed to memory, it's that Queen Bees Don't Eavesdrop. Or at least they don't get caught doing it.

Chapter Fifteen

No sooner had I enjoyed a hot shower and donned a fresh outfit of cotton capris and a roomy *Nobody Knows the Truffles I've Seen* T-shirt and had settled down to my breakfast of champions (leftover éclairs) than Sam popped her head into my kitchen.

"Look what I found." She shoved an Internet printout under my nose. "Ohio handgun laws," she said, as if I couldn't read the 18-point Times New Roman font at the top of the page.

"What about 'em?" I mumbled around a mouthful of chocolate crème-filled pastry nirvana. Seriously, I can't imagine a patisserie in all of Paris that makes better éclair's than Veralee Leinhart.

"It says here there's no state requirement that handgun buyers obtain a handgun license or undergo any type of safety training prior to buying a handgun. Read this." Sam used a well-manicured fingernail to tap at a paragraph for my reading pleasure.

The 10-point font in the body of the printout was a bit harder on my middle-aged eyes than the heading, but with my arms fully extended, I could make out the words. Barely. I read aloud. "There is no state requirement that a Brady criminal background check be done on people buying guns at gun shows if they are sold by private individuals or gun collectors. No records are required to be kept on gun show sales by private individuals or gun collectors, making it almost impossible for police to trace such weapons if they are used in a crime."

"And the CCW laws are even more generous."

"CCW?"

"Carrying a concealed weapon." Her voice indicated exasperation with my lack of gun-toting knowledge. She grabbed the printout from my hands and read. "Permits can be issued to anyone who can legally buy a gun and has undergone a modicum of training. They can then carry them in glove compartments or into playgrounds or restaurants." She tossed the papers onto the kitchen table. "So, are you thinking what I'm thinking?" she asked.

"That we need stronger gun laws?"

"No, that there are probably lots of guns being carried around Braddocks Beach without our knowledge. That's a scary thought." She used her crutch to nudge a chair away from the table and settled in while flipping the papers in front of me to another page. "But here's what I was looking for. Ballistic fingerprinting." Sam triple-tapped a paragraph in front of me.

I read aloud. "There are no state requirements that gun dealers or manufacturers provide police with sample bullets or digital images of bullets prior to the sale of a handgun, commonly known as ballistic fingerprinting, which would assist police in tracing bullets at crime scenes to the guns that fired them." I looked at Sam. "How is that good news?"

"The police probably haven't traced the gun that killed Reverend Hammersmith to our cat friend, Kat Adair, since it was a private sale. Which means we're one step ahead of them."

I reached for the phone on the counter behind me and handed it to Sam. "Why don't you call that tip in?"

She set the phone down on the table. "Already did."

"I don't believe you."

"Well, it doesn't matter, since we're five minutes from getting Reverend Hammersmith's killer locked away for life. You won't believe the anonymous tip I just received. Are you prepared to have your socks knocked off?"

I settled into the spindle-backed chair and prepared for my sports footies to fall right off my feet.

"Do you know Taffy Allen?"

"The church cleaning woman?"

Sam nodded.

I had seen Taffy Allen on many occasions. She reminded me of a small animal who expected a condor to scoop down and carry it off for its supper. With her job as the church cleaning woman, she was always shuffling along the hallways, dragging an ever-present trashcan on wheels behind her, in a weird, sneaky sort of way. Wait. Frisbee to the head moment. Taffy had been in a perfect position to see whoever snuck into Reverend Hammersmith's office and killed him. Why hadn't we thought of her earlier? Maybe because we weren't professional detectives. Not by any stretch of the imagination.

But Taffy could provide us all the answers. This was just the kind of break we'd been waiting for. I sat up straighter in my chair. "Do tell."

"Well, it's common knowledge that Taffy, who has not only taken care of the church for forty years, but has also cleaned Reverend Hammersmith's home for thirty-plus years, was the named beneficiary to the reverend's life insurance policy, seeing as how he didn't have any other family, and the policy was part of the benefit package and all."

"What are you saying here—"

Sam held up her hand. "Give me a minute. It occurred to me that if Taffy got antsy for the money, we might have a motive for murder, so I dug a little further and you'll never guess what?" She waited for me to guess.

I don't like playing games, so I said the first silly thing that popped into my head. "Taffy is the reverend's birth mother and she'd left him in the woods where he was found by a pack of wolves and raised as one of their own?"

"Really, Ellery. Don't be absurd. Reverend Hammersmith

is five years older than Taffy."

As if that's the part that bothered her, not the wolf part. "So what's the connection?" I asked.

"It seems Taffy had developed a bit of a gambling problem, and is into her Cleveland bookie for a whole lotta money. According to my sources, a guy named Guido paid Taffy a visit two weeks ago and," at this point Sam adopted a New York gangster accent, "treatened to break bote a' her legs if she didn't come up with fifty G's by de end a' da month."

"Now you're the one being absurd, Sam. You think that tiny woman managed to put a gun to Reverend Hammersmith's head, and he couldn't stop her?"

"Here's my theory. Maybe Taffy hadn't meant to kill him, only try to maybe get a loan out of him since he'd just inherited some money and all. Since she's the cleaning woman, she may have found the gun in a drawer or something and decided to use it to help persuade Reverend Hammersmith to help her out and the gun went off accidentally. That happens. I say it's worth asking her a few questions."

There was no doubt in my mind Taffy was not our killer. Don't ask me why, I just didn't "feel" it. But I did hold out hope she had seen whoever had done the dirty deed, so I agreed to drive Sam the three blocks over to Taffy's house. Not so much as agreed but conceded the point since chauffeuring duties in conjunction with Sam's investigation were part of the deal I'd made.

Taffy lived in a 1960s cape-cod-er on the fringes of Braddocks Beach proper. The house had, at one point, been painted a depressing shade of grey, if the remaining chips of paint were any indication. A collection of old rusty cars dotted the yard. In a word, depressing. It was obvious this woman was hurtin' for money. But kill for it? No way.

I pulled to the curb, but before I brought the vehicle to a complete stop, Sam had her car door open and crutches out. She was banging on the front door and calling "Yoo-hoo. Taffy," before I'd disengaged the car from my backside (*note to self, don't ever buy a car with bucket seats smaller than my bucket.*)

As I walked up the sidewalk, Sam's message became more frenetic, and less subtle. "Taffy, we know you killed Reverend Hammersmith. Now open up."

Uh oh. Subtlety had never been Sam's middle name.

"Back door!" Sam yelled to me, waving her crutches wildly toward the backyard. "She's making a break for it."

Hmm. I must have misjudged Taffy. Running is a sure sign of guilt. We needed to catch her before she got away. I looked around, but there was no back up to be seen. It was up to me to take down the killer before she escaped.

I veered to my right and galloped down the driveway as fast as an overweight woman with bad knees can gallop. Between the house and the detached garage stretched a yellow sheet hanging on the laundry lines. I caught sight of a pair of scrawny legs running behind the bed sheet.

Adrenaline fueled my muscles and I flew across the yard, ducked under the sheet and pounced on Taffy just before she hurdled over the sagging picket fence. I used my size to my advantage and smothered her body beneath mine, with the intent of holding her there until somebody with handcuffs arrived. No sound of sirens yet. What was taking Sam so long to call 9-1-1?

"Ellery, get off Taffy."

I looked over my shoulder and up at Sam. If looks could kill, I'd be deader than the proverbial doornail right now.

"Ellery, I said, get off Taffy. She didn't kill Reverend Hammersmith."

"Then why was she running? Only guilty people run. You said so yourself."

"I ran," Taffy mumbled from under me, "because the way Sam was banging on the door, I thought you were some, ah, friends of mine coming to collect the money I owe them."

"Taffy wasn't even in town on the day of Reverend Hammersmith's death," Sam explained. "I just remembered Thursdays are Taffy's day off work and she always goes to visit her sister in a nursing home up in Medina. I just received an answer to my text, confirming she was there all day." Sam flashed her cell phone screen at me, showing me a text message I couldn't read.

"Get off me, you big oaf," came the muffled voice from beneath me. "I can't breathe."

I rolled off Taffy and onto the dead grass that poked the soft, fleshy part of my bare arms. I stole a glance at Taffy. It was hard to tell if I'd done any damage to the small woman. Her hair, permed to within an inch of its life, was sticking out every which way, but it always stood out every which way. Her eyes had the look of cornered prey, but again, that was Taffy's everyday countenance. The scratch on her cheek looked fresh, but not dire. I didn't think she'd suffer much for having been tackled. Still, this was going to cost me another gift basket.

"I want to apologize for Ellery's behavior," Sam said, giving me one of her *Queen Bees don't Squish People* looks.

I knew that, of course. I'd been caught up in the heat of the chase, and made a mental note not to do it ever again.

"But I am partly to blame. I should have checked my sources first." Sam reached down and gave Taffy a hand up. "Please accept both Ellery and my apologies."

Sam and Taffy helped me to my feet. They brushed the grass off the places I couldn't reach then we wandered back across the yard in glacial silence.

"Let's sit for a bit." Sam motioned toward an old faded redwood picnic table that listed to the left, and we all settled in. "Taffy," Sam said. "I understand you're in need of some quick cash. Perhaps you have something you'd be willing to sell."

I surveyed the three rusty, abandoned vehicles lining the driveway. They were all on cement blocks, so not even a set of whitewalls worth buying. Nor was I interested in the mangled lawn rakes or the collection of cracked flower pots filled with dead daisies. I couldn't imagine anything inside her house being of value either.

"Do you still have that 624 Smith and Wesson?" Sam asked.

"The one Daddy gave me when Ronnie left?" Taffy asked back. "Sure do. Daddy wanted me to have protection against that rotten old drunk of an ex-husband after he threatened to kill me."

"How much?" Sam asked.

"Three hundred dollars. Firm."

"It sounds a bit high for a twenty year old pistol we don't even know works."

"It works. And I've got plenty of ammunition to go with it. Daddy wanted to make sure Ronnie was good 'n dead if he ever came sniffing around here again."

"Can we see it?" Sam asked.

This conversation was making me very, very nervous.

"I'll go get it." You'd a thought a firecracker had gone off underneath the table the way Taffy shot out of her seat and raced inside her house.

"Sam, what in the world do you want a gun for? They're deadly weapons."

"Might I remind you that guns don't kill people? People kill people. Besides, it's not for me, it's for you."

I had no desire to own a gun. "I believe I read somewhere that Queen Bees don't carry concealed weapons."

"They do if they need them for their own protection."

Before I could reply, a bullet whizzed past my nose.

Chapter Sixteen

"See, it works just fine." Taffy laid a vicious looking, wood-handled, brushed-stainless-steel barreled, snub-nosed gun on the table. A baggie full of bullets followed with an ominous clatter.

My heart slowly, very slowly, settled down into its natural rhythm as I choked against the odor of a smoking gun.

Sam picked up the evil-looking thing and inspected it, flashing the nozzle in my direction. There went my heart again. This time it thumped so hard I thought it had broken a rib. I rubbed the pain away.

"We're good, then. Contact Max for payment." Sam rose from her chair. "He's the one handling Ellery's finances right now."

Correction, I thought to myself. *Max allowed the trust to pay my food, clothing and shelter portion of my finances. I'm pretty sure a pistol doesn't fall into any of those categories.* I had never felt any compunction to share with Sam the details of Aunt Izzy's will. She was under the mistaken impression I inherited everything flat out. Frankly, it was none of her stinkin' business that I wouldn't see a cent for five years, if ever. But the way Sam was going around town spending money I didn't have, well, it had to stop. But this was not the time or the place to have a Come to Jesus meeting with Sam, so I kept my mouth shut. Hopefully Taffy offered a 30-day satisfaction guarantee policy.

Since Sam needed hands to maneuver her crutches, I

carried my new purchases to the Mini. I didn't like the heavy, cold and deadly feel of the gun in my hand. When we got to Sam's car, I tucked the pistol, barrel first, in the cup holder between the front seats and next to the snack-sized bag of Fritos. I couldn't help but smile at the novelty of an unopened bag of snack anything. I always opened them as soon as they were in my hands. Sam has a great deal more will power than I.

Once settled, we headed toward home. A quick trip on a clear day, but today we hit traffic at the Braddocks Beach government hub. Odd, that, as on sunny Saturday afternoons usually found most people, residents and tourists alike, hanging out on the beach.

"What's going on?" I slowed the car and rolled my window down so I could hear the speaker at the microphone.

A man's voice boomed over the temporary public address system, "Testing. Testing. One. Two. Three."

The city center just north of the tourist district consisted of a three-winged, four-story white-brick building at the top of wide open green space. It held a branch of the county library in the left wing, the police station on the right, and City Hall in the center.

Normally a Rockwellian scene filled with squirrels and birds and an occasional wayward sightseer stretched out on the lawn was different today. The veranda had been converted to a stage, with an official-looking podium and a cluster of microphones arranged between the pillars. A swarm of at least a hundred people gathered around.

"Stop," Sam ordered.

I'd already eye-balled a parking spot just ahead on Cowpens Street, but Sam hadn't meant stop and park, she meant stop and let her out right that second. Even though the car was still rolling, she swung her door open and had her crutches out. I slammed on the brakes. Sam exited and thumped the door shut behind her.

I parked and headed towards the crowd at a sedate pace. The green space was bigger than it looked from the street, and Sam was harder to catch up to than I expected, considering she only had one good leg. But she'd stopped at the edge of the stage and I managed to work my way through the crowd to be next to her. She brought me up to speed on her brief, but surprisingly thorough, reconnaissance.

"Press conference in ten minutes by Chief Lewis," she said, pausing to catch her breath. "He's going to announce the apprehension of a suspect in Reverend Hammersmith's murder."

I scanned the crowd and quickly identified two of the major news crews from the Cleveland area, based on the large decals on their humongous cameras. Their entourage, ranging from well-dressed reporters to torn jeans-wearing gaffers, wandered around the area. In contrast, the movers and shakers from the local government stood in quiet, stoic attention at the bottom of the steps. Local society members assembled in small groups, chatting and giggling as if this was some big ol' party.

Mystic Sayers jumped in front of Sam and me, snapping our picture with her professional-grade Nikon. "Any comments?" she asked us as she exchanged her camera for a tape recorder.

"No. We're still working on it," Sam replied, every bit the solicitous interviewee. "The police must know something we don't."

"Gee, ya think?" I snapped.

Sam flashed me a *Queen Bees Don't Make Snarky Remarks* look. She was right, of course. I really needed to think before snarking. I blamed it on low blood sugar. Breakfast was nothing but a distant (albeit delicious) memory and lunch didn't seem to be on the agenda anytime soon.

I leaned towards Mystic. "I'm glad this is over. I can go home and relax," I stated for the official record in my very best Queen Bee manner.

The microphones squeaked to life.

The crowd collectively turned their heads toward the stage and hushed.

Mayor Applewhite, looking every bit as dour as a pall bearer, took his place behind the podium. "Thank you all for attending today's press conference on such short notice. We thought it in the best interest of the town to disseminate the information as quickly and efficiently as possible."

Mayor Applewhite babbled on for five minutes, waxing poetic on Our Town that Time Forgot and bragging about how we have the lowest crime rate in the nation and nobody locks their doors. He quoted crime statistics dating back to the turn of the century. The twentieth century, that is.

I sure hoped the bad guys didn't read the Cleveland Plain Dealer or Braddocks Beach might experience a wave of burglaries.

"So, without further ado--"

Too late, Mayor. We'd already listened to too much "ado."

"--I turn the podium over to Braddocks Beach Police Chief Edward T. Lewis for the official statement."

"Based on that intro, my money's on an outsider," Sam said.

Chief Lewis cleared his throat and began speaking. "On Thursday, July fourteenth, at eleven fifty-nine a.m., Reverend Jonathon Thomas Hammersmith was shot through the head as he sat at his desk at the Braddocks Beach Church of Divine Spiritual Enlightenment. At eleven twenty-seven this morning we arrested Jefferson Scott Carter, age forty-five, on suspicion of murder. That's all I have to say at this time."

I looked at Sam to gauge her reaction, but she was gone.

"The citizens of Braddocks Beach don't pay you to arrest innocent people." That was Sam's voice coming through the speakers.

I looked up on stage, and there she was, standing on one

foot, resting on one crutch, and had the rubber tip of the other one pointed at Chief Lewis' Adam's apple. "Scott Carter is not a cold-blooded murderer. I've known him all my life."

"Yeah, you knew him, all right," yelled a voice from the crowd, and everyone joined in the bawdy laughter.

Mystic leaned over and whispered in my ear, "Sam's still carrying a torch for Scott, isn't she." It was more of a statement than a question.

"I don't know what you're talking about," I said to Mystic.

"Those two were an item from about second grade through high school. Sure bet they'd get married, but then Scott went off to college and came back with Melissa."

An item, huh? Based on the crowd's reaction, it had been an affair of the flesh as well as an affair of the heart. Sam's reaction to Bing's announcement made a whole lot more sense.

"Take back that statement you just made, Lewis," Sam's voice boomed over the speakers. "Or I'll make sure you're sued for false imprisonment. And then I'll serve your fat behind on a platter to the City Council and you can kiss this cushy job goodbye."

To say the silence was deafening would be akin to saying the Super Bowl was just another football game. Not even a robin dared chirp.

Chief Lewis slowly placed his hand on the crutch, and lowered it until it pointed at his thigh, but didn't let it go.

"We have indisputable evidence," he said.

"You've got nothing."

Out of the corner of my eye I saw Officer Compton unholster his Glock.

"I suppose you think that was Scott's gun he was killed with?" Sam said, drawing herself up to her full five feet of angry blond.

"We are working to ascertain the ownership of the

murder weapon."

"Let me save some of the taxpayer's money, Chief. Forget your He's-Guilty-Until-Proven-Innocent view of the law. Reverend Hammersmith owned that gun. He purchased it from Katherine Adair a week ago."

Judging by the Chief's reaction, this was news to him.

"The reverend needed it because he was being stalked..."

The chief's head snapped backwards as if Muhammad Ali himself had delivered an uppercut.

The crowd tightened around me.

"...and he wanted a gun to scare the person away. Instead, somebody used it to kill him. And it wasn't Scott Carter."

Chief Lewis dropped Sam's crutch.

The crowd surged, carrying me two feet closer to the stage.

"And how can you be so sure it wasn't?" A villainous sneer spread across his pasty face.

"I know for a fact your suspect did not have opportunity to splatter Reverend Hammersmith's brains because he and Bing Langstaff were intimately involved, that's how I know." Sam's announcement, amplified through the ten-foot high speakers, had been loud enough to be heard three counties over.

Sam had the good grace to look absolutely horrified that she'd just revealed Scott and Bing's secret to the world.

Chief Lewis looked as if someone had just let the air out of his balloon.

Mayor Applewhite turned a deathly shade of pale, then sank onto the platform's stairs and put his head between his knees.

The crowd started clucking like a yard full of chickens at feeding time.

"You've been holding out on me," Mystic screeched in my ear, then shoved her tape recorder in my face.

"Ms. Greene, you are under arrest for interfering with an official police investigation." Chief Lewis' statement, as well as the reading of her Miranda rights, were picked up by the microphone. He removed his handcuffs from his utility belt and snapped one on her wrist, and the other on his own before escorting the hobbling prisoner to the police station fifty yards away.

Mayor Applewhite stepped up to the microphone and announced, "On behalf of Chief Lewis, I want to withdraw the previous statement and apologize to Mr. Carter for any inconvenience or embarrassment this may have caused. The investigation into Reverend Hammersmith's murder will be reopened immediately." He turned and buzzed off like a fly who'd just spotted a flyswatter, the press following on his heels. Mystic was leading the charge.

I turned and scurried across the grass, worried that Mystic would lead the reporters to me once Mayor Applewhite refused to make any more comments for the record. One thing Mayor Applewhite excelled at was dodging reporters.

I made it all the way to Sam's car and had my hand on the doorknob, when a voice stopped me.

"I have a message for you, Ma'am."

I turned and saw Officer Compton approaching me.

"Ms. Greene said she'd be ever so grateful if you would take care of a few items for her," he said. "Since she'll be ah, how shall we say, out of commission for a while."

"What things?" I asked.

"She expects to use her one phone call to contact her attorney, and she asks that you call her husband and explain what happened, then get word to Miss Bing that she's terribly sorry about all this, that it all just slipped out without her thinking, and then ask Doris Rogers to call Melissa Carter and break the news to her before she learns of it through the grapevine. And Ms. Greene also asks that you send gift baskets around to Miss Bing, and the Carters and..." His voice trailed off. "What's that?" he asked, nodding in the direction of driver's seat of Sam's car.

"An unopened bag of Fritos. I know, weird, right? I mean, those things are meant to be eaten right away. Like right now." I reached through the window and grabbed the little orange-yellow bag and ripped it open. I held it out to Officer Compton. "Want some?

"No, not the Fritos. That," he said, with a suspicious emphasis on the word.

I looked over my shoulder. Taffy's gun lay in plain sight. "Oh, *that*. It's a gun."

"Is it yours?"

"Sort of." Since he didn't want the Fritos, I reached my hand into the package and helped myself.

"Do you have a permit to carry a weapon?"

"Not yet. We just bought it an hour ago."

"We?"

"Sam and me."

"I'm afraid I'm going to have to place you under arrest, Ma'am."

I swallowed the mushy wad of half-chewed Fritos. "Arrest? Me? What for?"

"It's against the law to carry a concealed weapon into a public area such as this without a permit," he said. He really was a sweet young man. He took the bag of chips from my hand, rolled the top down so they wouldn't go stale, and tucked them along the dashboard in a way they wouldn't spill, then slapped the cuffs on me and read me my Miranda rights.

No need to tell me to remain silent. I was too dumbfounded to speak.

Chapter Seventeen

"Ellery." Sam didn't sound surprised to see me when Officer Compton opened the cell door and led me in to the holding cell.

"Hey, Sam. Interesting press conference. Think Scott and Bing are going to appreciate you blabbing their affair to the world?" The Fritos hadn't kicked in yet so my blood sugar remained low, which made me testy. Or maybe being in this cold, depressing, run-down jail cell made me testy. I'd spent many long and lonely hours in this cell just last month. Worst night of my life. And I'd had some pretty bad ones.

"I feel terrible about that." Sam seemed sincere in her remorse. "But I couldn't let Scott be arrested for a murder he didn't commit, now, could I? I don't imagine he wanted Melissa to know where he'd spent his lunch hour, and I'm sure he didn't want to involve Bing, so he probably said he didn't have an alibi."

"Mystic wants to know if you still carry a torch for Scott."

Sam's reaction could best be described as pained. Whether painful memories, or painful remorse, or pain leftover from a broken heart, I couldn't discern.

"You never mentioned that part," I said before pursing my lips into an *I'm hurt you weren't totally honest with me* non-verbal message.

"Does one ever really get over their first love?" Sam sighed and leaned back on her cot. "So what are you in for? Did they get you for interfering with an official police investigation? I swear I didn't incriminate you."

"No, they saw Taffy's gun in the car."

That silenced her. For a long time. I climbed up to the top bunk, laid down and stared at the peeling ceiling. I was just about to nod off when Sam started talking.

"The police don't have any other leads on who killed Reverend Hammersmith."

"How do you know?"

"Because Chief Lewis asked me what other information we'd turned up regarding the murder. He wouldn't have asked if they had something of their own."

"What did you tell him?"

"The only remaining Helpful Bystander note from Reba's about the man in the plaid flannel shirt seen near the church dumpster at the exact time of the shooting. Seriously, that is the most useless bit of information. What motive could a homeless person possibly have? But now Lewis knows everything we know."

"You forgot about the possible motive of Reverend Hammersmith just coming into a lot of money."

"Oh, yeah."

"Don't get too excited. I used my one phone call to call George, who's going to call everyone else, including Max for me. And he wanted me to tell you he found out the amount of money Reverend Hammersmith inherited from his cousin was only a few G's, not millions, and it wasn't for the reverend, but would be in the form of a donation in his name to the food bank in Cleveland. So that money trail grew cold."

"Oh." Sam sounded deflated.

And knowing full well it would further deflate her, I needed to withdraw myself from this investigation. "I have faith in Chief Lewis, even if you don't. I say we leave killer-tracking to the professionals."

"Why should we give up now?"

"Because it doesn't seem right we're the ones in jail while

the killer runs free. Admit it, it's not our calling."

"I beg to differ. And considering I put my reputation on the line to solicit Titus' help in getting your family diaries out of the church's vault, you still owe me."

"Titus was your silver bullet?"

"I'm not at liberty to discuss the details, but I promise you'll have the diaries within the next forty-eight hours."

I recognized emotional blackmail when I saw it. Sam knew I wanted more than anything in this world to find out more about my heritage, specifically about my dad and why he left this town that he would have been King Bee of, or Top Dog, or whatever the male equivalent was. He would have done a much better job as societal leader than me.

But the reality was I am a Queen Bee currently locked in jail after having been coerced into helping Sam track down a killer. In a perfect world, Chief Lewis would manage to solve the case himself while Sam and I were detained in the Braddocks Beach jail, cellblock number two. Wouldn't that be nice?

My wishful thinking was interrupted by the sound of keys jangling. I looked towards the cell door and saw Officer Compton shoving a stooped over man to our cell. But when he raised his head I realized it was a she. Or a shadow of one. I think the lumberjack shirt and work boots were what had thrown me off. That, and the short, spiky, unwashed hair.

"Got you some company here."

Slam. Click. And then there were three. Quite possibly a record in the annals of Braddocks Beach crime history.

"Hello." Sam's voice sounded cheery despite our current depressing environment.

Our new cellmate nodded her head, then scuffled over to lean against the cinderblock wall.

"Here, come sit next to me." I heard Sam pat her cot.

Cellmate number three shook her head then slid to the floor. Her threadbare Dickies would be ineffective as a barrier between her scrawny backside and the cold cement.

"My name is Ellery Tinsdale," I said, tossing her my pillow, and that was a generous word for the two by two square of foam padding that smelled like decades-old hair tonic.

She smiled at me, then tucked it under her backside.

"I'm Samantha Greene," Sam said from her bunk. "And you are?"

"Libby. Libby Owens. From Lansing, Michigan."

As is true for everyone on this earth, Libby had a story, and with Sam's natural gift of drawing people out of their shells, we soon learned Libby's heartbreaking tale.

Our cellmate, who happened to be spending her fiftieth birthday in the slammer with us, had been a high school math teacher. But when a fourteen-year-old student accused her of seducing him, she'd been exiled from the profession. She'd quickly depleted her savings to cover legal fees, had lost faith in her community, and eventually had lost faith in herself. She'd been a street sleeper for three months now, moving south like a migrating bird in anticipation of winter. But here in Braddocks Beach, Reverend Hammersmith had given her the precious gift of hope. He'd found an attorney out of Detroit who had agreed to take Libby's case pro bono. Next Monday was the day the attorney would arrive to speak with her. But now without Reverend Hammersmith, without his contact (Libby didn't know the attorney's name), without his help in getting new clothes and a new look, and now with being incarcerated, she had no way of ever finding her way back to her old life.

"So, what are you in for, Libby? Did Chief Lewis catch you jaywalking or something?" Sam asked, not even attempting to make the snide remark sound sincere.

"No. They think I killed Reverend Hammersmith."

That had my attention. I rolled over in my bunk and studied our plaid-shirt wearing cellmate.

"Did you?" Sam asked.

"No," Libby said with sufficient conviction that I, for one, believed her. Seriously, the good reverend was the only person in the universe who was helping her out of her terrible circumstances, not to mention there was no way Reverend Hammersmith wouldn't have overpowered this wisp of a woman before she'd put the gun to his temple and pulled the trigger. She may have had opportunity, but nothing else.

But, wait…an amateur sleuth thought popped into my head (I hate it when that happens). If this woman hadn't killed Reverend Hammersmith, she might have seen who had.

"What can you tell me about Thursday at lunch time," I asked, having gone into full interrogation mode. "Did you see anyone suspicious going into or coming out of the church?"

"I don't know."

"Think," I said. "You may not realize you saw the killer."

Libby cocked her head to one side and seemed to give it serious though. "I'd been watching and waiting for Reverend Hammersmith at the back door. We'd developed a routine. Every day for the past two weeks I'd wait for him and he'd give me the uneaten half of his chicken salad sandwich on rye and a bag of chips. He said he was on a diet and hated to see it thrown away. He always delivered it with a smile and a quote. Last I saw him was Wednesday, and he said to me, 'There is surely a future hope for you, and your hope will not be cut off.'"

"Proverbs 23, verse 18," Sam said.

Libby bowed her head and seemed to be praying.

I took advantage of the moment of silence. Something Libby said had set my mental gears moving. I stretched out on my bunk, crossed my ankles, tucked my hands behind my head, and thought through some details. Sam and I—as well as the rest of Braddocks Beach—were aware of the reverend's daily routine to walk to Tinky's for lunch (hence the window of opportunity for our little breaking and entering episode) at 11:45 every day, and now we know he had developed the habit of bringing the uneaten half of his sandwich to Libby. He always dined at Tinky's, always the same booth at the front window overlooking merchant circle. I didn't know much about Reverend Hammersmith, but I know he was fascinated by human nature, and his favorite pastime was people watching, be it from Tinky's window or on a bench in the park or from his place in the pulpit.

The day of his death he'd been eating at his desk, a fact brought to mind much too vividly when I recalled Sam mentioning his chicken salad sandwich having looked like it had been splattered with ketchup. What had altered his routine on Thursday? And if he hadn't gone out for lunch, how did he come to have lunch at his office? Had he brought it from home? Had he gone out early and come back with it? Or had it been delivered? And would the delivery have included a side order of a fatal bullet?

Chapter Eighteen

George hadn't made his sunset deadline, but had managed to have all three of us sprung from the pokey by sunrise on Sunday morning. He'd posted Libby's bond, paid Sam's $150 fine for misdemeanor interference with a police investigation, and produced a permit in my name to carry a concealed weapon so the charges against me were dropped. Someone had connections somewhere to get the paperwork pushed through that fast. I didn't ask, and George didn't tell.

The Mini Cooper was where we'd left it on Cowpens Street, but the gun had gone missing. I hoped it was in safe hands, especially since my fingerprints were all over it. I made a mental note to contact Officer Compton to confirm he'd taken it into police custody.

We three jailbirds piled into Sam's car, and I drove us the few short blocks home. We planned to clean up and head out for a celebratory breakfast and to plan Libby's future in Braddocks Beach. Sam had decided Libby would be the perfect Pygmalion Project for me, as apparently Queen Bees should always be involved in some sort of social cause. I'd been here a month and had yet to do anything for anyone other than myself.

"You look mah-velous," Sam said an hour later as a new and improved Libby danced down the grand staircase to the first level of my house that had so many genuine 1800s antiques that it felt more like a museum to me than a home.

I agreed with Sam. Libby did look ever so much better, freshly scrubbed and wearing a cotton, button-down dress in a dandelion yellow color that complimented her sandy blonde hair and drew out her soulful brown eyes. The clothes and ballet slippers were courtesy of Sam's closet. Libby was at least six inches taller than Sam, but probably weighed ten pounds less. How much she *didn't* weigh boggled my mind.

"Thanks. To both of you," Libby said as she hit the bottom step and did a pirouette. "I'm not sure I'll ever be able to repay your kindness."

"No need." Sam waved off the gratitude. "Now, who's up for breakfast at Tinky's? My treat."

No need to ask me twice. I led the way out the door.

Sam insisted she could make the two blocks on crutches, since it was a beautiful morning to be outside. Too bad her feet didn't move as fast as her mouth. The pace seemed painfully slow, amplified since I never had eaten any dinner the previous night.

Sam planned Libby's future. "We'll find you a job, right here in town. How does that sound?"

Libby nodded her head like a child agreeing to be good in exchange for a cupcake.

"Ellery owns a couple of cabins down by the lake. I'm sure she'll let you stay there."

That was news to me. To be honest, I didn't have a full grasp on what all I owned. Or would own, when the inheritance finally came my way. I really should have a set-down with Max and get my head wrapped around the whole thing, and then a set-down with Sam to get her to stop being so generous with things I didn't own. Especially money.

"You can stay there rent free until you get on your feet," Sam continued settling Libby's affairs. "The summer tourist season is in full swing, and there are jobs aplenty to be had, if you don't mind hard work."

"Don't mind it at all."

"Until we get a job lined up, you can help Ellery and me

help the police figure out who killed Reverend Hammersmith. Frankly, we're are at a dead end, no pun intended, and maybe you can give us a fresh perspective, since you were hanging around the church for the past few weeks."

"I sure hope I can be of assistance." Sam and Libby hugged again.

Henrietta Zucker—sporting Pineapple Passion-colored hair--and her canine companion Pipsqueak Rapscallion Zucker were speed walking in the opposite direction. Henrietta paused to exchange a few pleasantries. I used the opportunity to have a chat with Pipsqueak, who since he had been a guest at my house for a few days last month was the only canine on earth with whom I was on speaking terms. And only then because he had saved my life.

With a final pat on his wiry head, he and Henrietta were off, and we were on our way to Tinky's.

"Isn't that exciting," Sam asked.

"What?"

"What Henrietta just told us about—"

Sam didn't have the opportunity to finish sharing Henrietta's exciting news, because as we approached the corner of Yorktown and Tinsdale, the body of a teenage boy flew in front of us and right into oncoming traffic.

Libby raced into the street and stopped the cars. Were it not for the quick actions of our new friend, he would have been squished flatter than a granola bar that had been in the bottom of a third-grader's backpack for five weeks. She'd just saved the young boy's life.

I stood glued to my spot, waiting for my stunned brain to process the event and form a course of action.

"Ellery, do something," Sam said, her cell phone already to her ear.

Leave it to Sam's brain to do the thinking for me.

I stepped into the intersection and knelt by the boy's

writhing form. The red-headed, freckle-faced youth was losing the battle against tears, which started in earnest when I reached out to calm him. He cradled his left arm to his chest and rocked back and forth. My non-medical but plenty of playground supervising diagnosis was a broken collar bone.

"It's okay," I said. "Help is on the way." And it was. I heard the sirens in the distance. "What's your name?"

"Brandon Pelletier."

"Can you tell me what happened?"

"Eff-in hydrant."

I looked toward the sidewalk, and sure enough, there lay the red Schwinn bicycle used by Tinky's delivery boys. The patriotically-painted fire plug showed no signs of damage.

"How many fingers am I holding up?" I held up my hand in front of his face.

"Four," he said.

Uh oh. Could be a concussion.

"And one thumb," he added with a weak smile.

Ha ha. Like I hadn't heard that one a gazillion times in my tenure as an elementary school teacher, but I smiled anyway, for his benefit. Maintaining a sense of humor bode well for a speedy recovery.

"Hey, Brandon," Sam spoke over my shoulder.

"Hey, Mrs. Greene."

"Did you deliver lunch to Reverend Hammersmith on Thursday?"

What did Sam think she was doing, asking questions like that at a time like this?

Before Brandon could reply, we were shoved out of the way by medics with enough equipment to treat a large-scale catastrophe. They were soon joined by a barefoot and braless woman wearing only an oversized sleep shirt that kept her just this side of indecent exposure.

"That's Honey, Brandon's mom," Sam told me. "I called

her before I called nine-one-one."

"Do me a favor," I said as I lifted the bike to an upright position. "If I'm ever in trouble, call the emergency folks first."

"Honey had a lot further to travel."

I doubted I would ever truly understand Sam's logic process.

We maintained our curbside position as the crowd grew behind us. The paramedics had more trouble treating Honey, who had sliced her foot open during her barefoot race to be with her son, than they did Brandon. In less than twenty minutes, the two were loaded onto gurneys. The crowd broke out in applause as the latest episode of the Braddocks Beach reality show ended.

"Wait." Sam waved her crutch toward the paramedics.

But the paramedics didn't wait. The procession rolled toward the back of the ambulance.

"Cover for me. I'm going in," Sam whispered, ventriloquist style.

"Huh?"

"I need to ask Brandon if he delivered Reverend Hammersmith's lunch on Thursday. That's his route, and it makes sense if Reverend Hammersmith didn't go to Tinky's, then Tinky's went to him. Maybe he saw the killer. I need you to create a diversion of some sort so I can ask him."

I had to give credit to Sam, she sure could come up with a plan when a plan was needed quickly. All I had to do was create a diversion of some sort.

Without thought to the consequences, I swung my leg over the seat of the red Schwinn and pushed off into the street with a plan of intercepting the gurney before it was loaded. The front rim had been damaged in Brandon's run-in with the hydrant, so the bike was wobbly. I hadn't ridden a bike in forty plus years, so I was wobbly. Add the gravitational pull of a downhill slope and the effect was less steady than a baby's first steps.

And with equally undesired results.

I crashed into a police car and flew over the handle bars with a whole lot less finesse than Brandon had shown. Fortunately I was not hurt, mostly because a young policewoman cushioned my fall.

She, unfortunately, slammed her head against the side mirror of the police car on her way down and was rendered unconscious.

The paramedics raced the ten feet and tended to us immediately. They diagnosed me with a contusion on my left cheek, which sounded much worse than it was. More disturbing by far was the realization that my new Adidas warm up suit had been shredded at the knees.

Officer Taylor regained consciousness quickly, but was loaded into the ambulance with Brandon and his mom as a precaution.

"You'll want to send a gift basket," Sam said as she lifted the bike upright.

"You're the one who told me to create a diversion. You send it." I brushed road grime from my backside.

"By 'diversion,' I didn't mean for you to practically kill someone. Why can't you just faint like a normal person?"

"Women stopped fainting when fashion stopped dictating they wear corsets tightened to a 13-inch waist. And amen to that!"

"Some women still do faint. You might want to work on that. It comes in handy in sticky situations." Sam pushed Brandon's bike, now with a torqued fender and bent wheel rim, to the curb where Libby sat waiting for us.

I followed and we continued our way along the sidewalk to Tinky's.

"What did you find out?" I asked.

"I'll get to that in a minute, but I wanted to finish telling you Henrietta Zucker's news," Sam said. "Porter Trawbridge, he's a Newbee, by the way." Sam gave Libby a quick recap of the social hierarchy here in Braddocks Beach. "Porter's the nicest guy in the world. Too shy by half, but will make a great catch for some lucky girl. And he'll be fighting them off with a stick once he turns in the winning ticket for Monday's Classic Lotto drawing. The jackpot was seven-point-nine million. Can you believe it?"

"No, I can't, because if he'd won it would be in the news. You have to sign off on publicity when you win." Not that I was an authority, but I had played regularly and had studied the rules for claiming a prize in the event my numbers came up. I always like to be prepared.

"He hasn't turned the ticket in yet. It's locked up in a safety deposit box until Porter can consult a tax specialist. Uncle Sam will want his share, of course. Sometimes, especially as young as Porter is, the annual payout instead of the lump sum is the better option."

We reached our destination only to find a line out the door and halfway down the block. Sam worked her magic and got us head-of-the-line privileges. We were seated in a back booth within minutes.

"How'd you do that?" I asked as soon as we were settled.

"It's not who you know, but what you know. I've got some dirt on Tinky that will ensure I have a table for the rest of my life."

"Oh, do tell," Libby said, a mischievous twinkle lighting her hallowed eyes.

"I'd tell you, but then I'd have to kill you." Sam winked at Libby, who laughed at Sam's joke. I knew Sam was serious. Dead serious. Sam's clout in this town came from her knowledge of every skeleton hanging in every resident's closet. How she discovered the secrets lurking behind the white picket fences of Braddocks Beach didn't bear thinking about.

We ordered. Where Libby thought she would tuck away a

six-pack of pancakes, three eggs, bacon, sausage, ham and hash browns I didn't have a clue. I ordered the same, but felt confident I had the stomach to meet the challenge.

We sipped strong coffee while Sam brought Libby up to date on our quest to find Reverend Hammersmith's killer.

"Did Brandon tell you anything helpful?" I asked as soon as the facts of the case, of which there were disappointingly few, had been shared.

"I have more questions now than I did before," Sam answered. "He said that Reverend Hammersmith had called at nine that morning to arrange for his order to be delivered to him at noon. Apparently, he had a lunchtime appointment."

"Janet Staunton?"

"That's my guess. We'll confirm it when we peek at his personal calendar. Anyway, Brandon said he went out to get on his bike and found it had two flat tires and saw two kids running away. He went inside and told Tinky what had happened, and a guy paying his bill at the register said he was just heading that way and would be happy to deliver the reverend's lunch."

"Brandon didn't know him?"

Sam shook her head.

Our breakfasts arrived, and we all focused on the task at hand. Good food. Good conversation. Good coffee. I was happy.

By the time we'd all cleaned our plates, Sam had spoken to Tinky himself and Libby had been hired as a fill-in delivery person, effective immediately, until Brandon was fit to resume his duties.

Things were working out for everyone.

For almost everyone, that is.

For one resident of Braddocks Beach, things had taken a deadly turn.

Chapter Nineteen

We're going to have to put our investigation on hold for a few hours," Sam said as if she were the police commissioner herself, and not some nosy friend of the deceased.

But no matter, I liked the sound of that. An entire afternoon to relax.

"We've got to head down to the property on the southern tip of the lake. You promised Max you'd give him your decision by tomorrow morning."

The property in question was a woodsy hundred acres complete with two miles of shoreline on Lake Braddock's southeastern edge. At one time it had been a private summer retreat for one of Cleveland's elite during the railroad boom, but it had been abandoned when the owner busted during the depression. The house had burned to the ground more than sixty years ago. I'm still fuzzy on how it came into the Tinsdale holdings.

Aunt Izzy had been approached about selling the acreage before her untimely demise and Max asked my opinion if I wanted to hang on to it or let it go. Either way, no money for me for the four years and eleven months remaining on the time stipulated in the will, but at least Max was giving me some input on the decisions. I was leaning toward selling, preferring cash to real estate I'd never use. But this was my first major financial decision, and I couldn't make it sight unseen.

"I'm too tired to go today," I told Sam.

"Tired? From what?"

"From a bad night's sleep in a cold jail, on the heels of a bad night's sleep in your cramped car after a completely sleepless night while we made the picture frames. You know I need a full eight hours. We'll go tomorrow."

"Max needs your decision by tomorrow. The offer expires at ten a.m., and you've put this off for a month already."

Sam was right. I hated it when Sam was right, which was always.

"Let's go," she said, channeling her inner cheerleader. "I dropped my car off this morning to get some work done and George took his to his class reunion at Mt. Union, so we'll have to take that new conveyance of yours."

I noticed Sam couldn't bring herself to call it a car either. "It's only street legal for roads with a speed limit under twenty-five miles per hour."

"No problem. The utility road is the most direct route there, and your conveyance will be better than a car."

"How long will we be gone?"

"A couple of hours. We'll be home before dark."

"What about lunch?"

"You just ate enough to keep a small African village alive for a week."

"That was because I didn't get dinner last night on account of you bought a gun that I got caught carrying." Guilt can work both ways.

"Okay, tell you what. Doris dropped off a plate of food from last night's potluck at the concert in the park. I'll pack that up and you can eat it when you get hungry."

Food, especially Braddocks Beach homemade potluck food, was a powerful motivator for me. I agreed to the plan.

Twenty minutes later, I had donned the only hiking attire I owned; tattered, splattered jeans, a stretched out T-shirt the color of recycled dog food, and an old pair of seriously stained Keds. This outfit also doubled as my housecleaning attire, my gardening attire, and my painting attire. It was as far removed from Queen Bee attire as one could get.

Sam arrived looking less like a hiker and more like an afternoon tea attendant. She'd changed into a flowing floral-print dress and had thrown a lightweight sweater over her shoulders, topping it off with three strands of pearls. She wore one beige pump, and accessorized her outfit with purple toes peeking out of the ACE bandage on the other foot.

I slid behind Peep's wheel and Sam settled in the shotgun seat. A foil-wrapped Chinet plate rested on the floor in the backseat and two bottles of Snapple sat in the cup holders. I felt adequately prepared for a few hours sojourn into the wilderness. The sun was high, the sky was blue, and I found myself looking forward to communing with nature, but I would never in a million years let Sam know that.

The utility road broke off the beach road just south of town. It was wide enough, and paved at the beginning. But once we passed the various and sundry signs warning off unlawful trespassers, the lane diminished to nothing more than an overgrown footpath, and that was a generous term. But the little golf cart had the heart and soul of an F-150, and we ploughed along, five miles, uphill. There was plenty of communing with nature along the way. Too much, actually, with all manner of biting bugs that seemed attracted to Sam's bug spray rather than repelled. We scared off a few hundred squirrels, startled a number of rabbits, and even had one deer sighting. Well, the tail of the deer. Those are some fleet-footed critters.

After about forty-five minutes we arrived at a clearing. I hadn't expected it to be quite this tranquil. Or this isolated. Or to find somebody had beaten us there.

"Whose truck is that?" I asked Sam as I pulled up next to an Explorer. I couldn't tell the color through all the dirt.

"That's Porter Trawbridge's work truck. Wonder what he's doing up here. Is he the buyer?"

"Max didn't mention any names."

"Maybe this is how he's going to spend his lotto millions. Yooo-hooo. Pooorrrrterrr," Sam sang out.

But the only response was a skittering noise in the pile of leaves near my feet.

"He might be off hiking. Let's go ahead and take a look around. I haven't been here in years."

"When were you ever here?"

"It's a rite of passage to spend Halloween night senior year camped here. The area is supposedly haunted."

"By whose ghost?"

"Nobody knows for sure. There's no record of anyone ever having died here, but all kinds of mysterious lights and close encounters of the unexplainable kind have occurred. Maybe this was an old Indian burial ground or something."

"Was there any Tequila involved in these camping trips?"

"No, of course not. Well, not Tequila. Maybe a little Mad Dog."

"What's that?"

"Really cheap wine. Tastes like cough syrup."

So young Sam did have a little rabble-rouser in her. There was hope for her after all. "Did you make it?"

"Make what?"

"The whole night without getting scared and going home?"

"Of course."

But her "of course" carried the undertones of "not even fifteen minutes."

We walked the few remaining yards to the edge of a cliff, and I stopped walking and breathing. The view was nothing short of spectacular. Lake Braddock stretched across 39,000 acres, its blue waters dotted with a few tiny daysailers. The lake was surrounded by miles of unsullied shoreline. The cluster of buildings directly across from us was the town of Braddocks

Beach. I didn't know who owned the rest of the land, maybe me, maybe somebody else who didn't want to see nature spoiled--or didn't need the millions of dollars the sale of it would bring.

We stood on the southeast part of a private cove, and followed the cliff line further south. I turned and gazed out across the water again, thinking for a minute I had died and gone to heaven because this represented the peacefulness, solitude and natural beauty I hoped the afterlife held. "This must look spectacular in the fall."

"It does."

We walked further uphill and then across a vast expanse of hip-high weeds and stopped at the base of a charred foundation. The old summer house. "This wasn't a cottage, it was a mansion," I said. The single story foundation had to have been 10,000 square feet, minimum. And if it had been two or three stories tall, well, the math boggled my mind.

"You assumed summer house meant cottage. It was a very large home that hosted very large summer parties for Cleveland's elite. Remind me to show you a picture when we get home. Yooo-hooo. Pooorrrrterrr," Sam called again. "I wonder where he is."

"Is he a hunter?"

"Not to my knowledge."

"Then I'm sure he didn't go far."

I left Sam slouched on her crutches while I retraced my steps to the water's edge and looked down at the small, private cove surrounded by the fifty-feet-high cliffs. Not rocky cliffs, but an unstable combination of soft clay and sand. If anyone planned to settle this bit of paradise then a retaining wall would be required.

I stepped closer to look down at the water lapping against the steep walls. My foot slipped, then the earth crumbled under me. I gave out a small shriek--small might be an understatement--and fell back on my rear end. The earth stopped moving. My heart started beating again. I peered over my feet to the breeze-driven water lapping softly below. I probably wouldn't have been killed, but a broken neck wasn't outside the realm of possibility.

"Do you see Porter?" Sam called.

It occurred to me the berm could have crumbled on him, and he could be lying down there in need of assistance. I swung my legs around so that I was stretched out on my belly, then slithered to the edge and peered over. No beach. Just cliff meeting water. But no sign of a lifeless body floating face down, thank goodness. "Nope. Nobody here."

I could hear Sam's sigh of relief echo my own.

"Come away from there before you fall in."

Now that was the first sensible thing Sam had said all day. I scootched backwards, sat up, caught my breath, brushed myself off, and with great effort, pushed myself to my feet in the ungainly way of a camel and started walking up the hill toward Sam.

It was then that I saw it. Two slit eyes and a forked tongue, eyeballing me as it slithered by. Close by. Close enough that it could bite me. Only I wasn't going to give it an opportunity. I jumped backwards, and off the cliff.

I yelled all the way down.

I yelled after I landed in the water, mostly because the sound of my voice assured me I was still alive.

I yelled after Sam poked her head over the edge and asked if I was okay, mostly because I was mad at myself.

I yelled when I realized my cell phone was of no use since it was now soaking wet, and that Sam had left hers at home on the charger.

I yelled while we tried to figure out the best way for me to get from the bottom of the cliff to the top. A few attempts at climbing up crumbling clay and tumbling back to the water had me feeling like Sisyphus.

And then I yelled on and off for the next hour while Sam

buzzed back to town. To my way of thinking, yelling kept the flesh-eating critters away, and would bring Porter Trawbridge looking, if he happened to wander back to his truck.

There wasn't anything in the way of beach here, so my feet were submerged in three inches of chilly lake water while I rested my back against the cliff. The clay I leaned against was cold, and I was cold. And wet. And all that yelling had made me thirsty. And hungry. Had I been thinking clearly, I would have had Sam toss me the food and Snapples before she'd left.

"Ellery?"

Sam had returned! I popped up and turned to greet my saviors. "That was quick." Only one curly blond head peered over the edge.

"Small problem, here."

"How small?"

"Pretty big, actually."

"How big?"

"The vehicle died about a half-mile down the path."

Oh.

"I think the battery's dead."

Dang. It hadn't even occurred to me to keep an eye on the juice level while driving out here. All that cross country terrain must have taken its toll.

"And I'm not able to walk five miles on crutches. I barely made it back here."

Double dang.

"But I think I have a plan. If you swim out of the cove and head south, the hill slopes down enough you can hike up here."

"How far do I have to swim?" I looked down at my jeans and T-shirt and Keds. I wasn't a strong swimmer to begin with, and wet jeans would make it downright difficult. Drowning was not the way I intended to leave this earth.

"Once you get around the cove there's a beach you can

walk along until the hill slopes down."

"So I just have to swim around the cove?"

"Yup."

"Then walk how far?"

"Maybe a mile."

"And then a mile back to where you are."

"Uphill."

Like I needed to hear that part. Sigh. And I hadn't trained for a biathlon in oh, about, never. "How 'bout if we just wait for Porter to show up?"

"If he were here, we'd have seen him by now. The only thing I can figure is his truck broke down and he called somebody to come get him. I know Titus planned to take his nephew's Cub Scout troop to the Cleveland Zoo today, and they won't be back until after dinner. I don't imagine he'll be out to hook 'er until tomorrow."

I shivered against the thought of spending a night in the water with my wet clothes and calculated hypothermia would set in about two-seventeen a.m. "Is Titus the only tow truck driver in town?"

"Yup."

"Did you tell George where we are?"

"I haven't talked to George since yesterday when he took off for his fraternity reunion at Mount Union College, remember?"

Great. Just great. "Can you throw me down my Snapple before I take off? I'm really thirsty."

Sam didn't answer.

"Sam?"

"Yeah?"

"Snapple?"

"I couldn't very well carry food and drinks while on crutches, could I?"

Great. Stuck miles from civilization with no food or

drinks—and the lake water in which my feet were submerged didn't count as it was too lake-y for my drinking standards--and me soaked to the skin.

"How long before you think anyone will realize we're missing?"

"Doris Rogers might notice there aren't any lights on at either of our houses tonight and get suspicious, but I doubt she comes looking for us out here. She might call George, but I don't know if he'll remember I said we planned to come visit the property. He has selective hearing issues."

I weighed my options against the weight of my wet jeans. "So, I just swim around that part sticking out there and then on the other side there will be a beach and I can walk a mile and climb up the hill and then hike back to where you are and then what?"

"And I'll have a nice campfire waiting for you and you can dry off and we'll have ourselves a little camp out. I feel certain Titus will come get Porter's truck first thing in the morning."

I let out a sigh so deep there wasn't one molecule of carbon dioxide left in my lungs. If my life got any better, I'd have to hire someone to help me enjoy it.

Chapter Twenty

By the time I returned to the old summer homestead, Sam had the makings of a campfire. She'd cleared a small area of brush and assembled rocks around a stack of pine needles and twigs. A pile of larger pieces of wood stood nearby, ready to add once the tinder was ablaze. She deserved a Girl Scout badge for campfire assembly. She failed, however, to deliver on the actual roaring fire aspect of things.

"I didn't have any matches," she explained as I plopped my weary bones next to her on the bumper of Porter's truck. "And rubbing two sticks together is nothing but an old wives' tale."

I'm not sure which one of us was closer to tears.

"No sign of Porter or Titus either, I take it?"

"Nope."

"I don't suppose you found any berries or anything we could eat?"

"I'm a housewife, not a survivalist, Ellery." Sam's shoulders dropped and her head fell forward and she started shrinking right before my very eyes. I thought for a moment she might melt into a puddle of water like the Wicked Witch of the West. "I'm sorry, El," she whispered in a tiny, tired voice. "I shouldn't take my frustrations out on you. I'm tired and cold and angry and frustrated."

"Me too."

She lifted her head, squared her shoulders and I saw a spark of the Sam I'd come to know. "How was your hike back?"

"Beyond the most miserable experience you can imagine.

Treacherous. Slow-going. Buggy. Arduous. Scratchy. Soggy." I paused to think up more adjectives, but it required more mental energy than I had left in me. "It took so long my clothes are almost dry." The outerwear, anyway. I'd stopped and discarded the innerwear before I'd headed uphill, leaving my granny panties hanging on a low-hanging branch. Wet undies make me full-on crazy, and I was already three-quarters there without that aggravation.

"I don't suppose you want to hike back to town and get help?"

I almost laughed at the hopeful tenor in her voice. "No, I don't suppose I do. It's almost dark. I've been rode hard and put away wet, as the old adage goes. And I haven't had so much as an M&M since breakfast at Tinky's. What do you think the chances are Porter has a Snickers bar in his glove compartment? I'd give my right arm for a Snickers or a Kit Kat bar right now."

"Porter's more of a peanut butter cracker guy."

"Works for me." Actually, I was a little embarrassed I hadn't thought about it sooner.

I scurried around to all the doors on Porter's Explorer, only to find them all locked. Seriously, here in the middle of the wilderness? When nobody locked their vehicles back in town? I peered in the window hoping to find something edible, preferably from the chocolate food group. Nope. The backseat held an assortment of tools of the carpenter's trade, and a large bulky tarp wrapped in yards of clothesline. It could be a tent, which would give us shelter for the night. But then again, if we were to get the truck opened I'd much rather curl up inside the vehicle than out. Be it for food or shelter, we needed to get the truck opened.

"Help me find a rock," I said to Sam. "I'll break a window."

"Ellery Elizabeth Tinsdale. You will not, under any circumstances, violate another person's property."

"I suppose you'd rather sleep on the ground, with snakes

slithering over you and raccoons nibbling at your toes?"

Sam looked horrified at the thought. "Maybe he has a hidden key or something."

While Sam crawled around the truck, sticking her hands in every crevice she could find, I picked up one of the larger rocks from around her fire pit. It was about the size of a loaf of bread and as heavy as a sack of potatoes. Perfect. I balanced it on my shoulder while she conducted her search.

Nothing. She refused to let me break a window. I returned the rock to its place around where the roaring fire should be, but as soon as Sam sneaked off to answer the call of nature, I picked it up and sent it sailing through the backseat window. I was happily stretched in the reclined passenger seat when she returned.

She didn't say a word, simply leaned her crutches against the side of the truck and slipped into the empty driver's seat.

I opened the bin between the seats, and lo and behold, an unopened package of cheese on wheat crackers. "It's our lucky day," I said, offering her one.

She accepted. "Thanks."

I gobbled down the five remaining crackers. Everything I needed to know about sharing I'd learned in kindergarten.

The canopy of trees shut out the evening sunlight and darkness descended. The night sounds crescendoed. And Sam caught her second wind.

"Let's go over everything we know about Reverend Hammersmith's murder."

"Okay. Let's see. Hmm. How's this. We don't know one dang thing."

"If you'd rather not discuss the murder, I suppose we could sing campfire songs."

Before she could launch into the first verse of *Make New Friends*, I said, "Or here's an idea. We could sleep." I hunkered down in my seat.

"I can't sleep. Not with all the ghosts floating around here."

"They only exist in your imagination."

A ghostly sound carried through the shattered backseat window.

"What was that?" Sam clutched my arm, her French-tipped nails piercing the tender flesh.

"Ouch. Stop it." I smacked her hands away. "It's an animal or something."

"I've never heard an animal wail like that before."

Honestly, I hadn't either. I refused to think about the other possibilities. We both needed to keep our minds focused on something else. "Okay, let's talk murder."

We came up with a probable timeline of events as we knew them.

Reverend Hammersmith felt he was in danger. He'd purchased a gun from Kat Adair as a deterrent should the situation ever get sticky. According to Sam, he'd been wearing one of those over the shoulder holsters the way undercover guys do. An image of a heat-packing preacher gave me the giggles.

Janet Staunton had come to town to tell Reverend Hammersmith of her bequest, and maybe in the hope of rekindling a fifty-year-old romance, but that was pure romantic conjecture on Sam's part. Since Janet, too, was dead, we had no way to confirm or deny that.

The reverend had ordered his lunch instead of walking the two blocks to Tinky's so that he wouldn't miss his appointment. The meeting could have been with Janet, or it could have been with just about anyone else in the entire world.

Brandon could not make the delivery because his bike had two flat tires. Instead, a person of interest--as Sam, an avid *Castle* fan, labeled him--delivered the lunch.

Sometime between the delivery of lunch and the arrival of Janet, someone else had shown up and we both knew what happened. Given the spooky setting for our conversation, we skipped over the gory details from which ghost stories spring.

So we focused on who we knew had not killed Reverend Hammersmith.

The killer was not the illegitimate son of Janet and the reverend. He was out of the country healing sick children in third-world nations.

The killer was not the person we mistook for the illegitimate son of Janet and the reverend. He didn't even know Reverend Hammersmith.

The killer was not Bing Cherry Langstaff. She was otherwise occupied in an intimate rendezvous with Scott Carter.

Neither was the killer Scott Carter, as he was intimately involved with Bing Langstaff.

Nor was the killer Melissa Carter, because she'd been busy volunteering at the Blood Mobile.

The killer was not insurance beneficiary Taffy Allen, who had alibied out, having been with her handicapped sister in Medina.

The killer was not the shifty-eyed character spotted behind the church, because that was the homeless Libby. While she had no alibi, she did not have the heart, nor the strength, of a killer.

Looking at it from another angle, a firebug had set off explosions at the manse. Perhaps whoever was stalking Reverend Hammersmith had hoped to incinerate any notes or files that would incriminate someone. The question was, who?

The police did not seem to be any closer to finding a killer themselves, despite whatever forensic evidence they had at their disposal.

But they didn't have Sam. I had no doubt she would hound, bully, pester and threaten every citizen of Braddocks Beach in order to find out which one was hiding a terrible secret. My worry was the collateral damage, like Bing. How many other lives would be destroyed in her poking her button nose where it didn't belong?

"We have a long list of who didn't do it," I said once we'd each spent a while mulling over the facts. "Do we have any names at all of maybe who did do it?"

"I can't think of a single person in Braddocks Beach. It must be someone from outside. Something in Reverend Hammersmith's past. After all, old secrets cast long shadows. Who knows what kind of things he witnessed while traveling with the carnival back when he was a teenager."

"But how are we ever going to retrace a probably now-defunct carnival's trail a half-century ago?"

Silence stretched between us. The creatures of the night seemed to have settled down. My eyelids felt like they had sandbags attached to them.

I was somewhere in that shadowy state between awake and asleep when I heard the muffled sounds of "Bohemian Rhapsody". For a moment I thought I was dreaming. And then I realized it was a cell phone. In the cargo area of the truck.

Praise the Lord and pass the potatoes--we were saved!

Chapter Twenty-One

The ringing stopped before I hopped out of the truck and opened the lift gate to the cargo area. I couldn't discern the phone's exact location, but I knew it was back there, buried somewhere in the mess. Nothing as easy as it lying there in plain sight.

We started our search with the obvious areas; under the seats, in the tool box, in the old-school metal lunchbox (alas, only filled with empty baggies, a mere reminiscence of meals past) and the storage bins. Then we moved on to less likely but still possible storage places; the discarded boots, the plastic bag filled with plastic bags, and a sack full of library books (Porter was an aficionado of pulp westerns.) At the bottom of the bag I found an OSU Buckeyes sweatshirt. Once I ascertained the pockets didn't contain anything hard and heavy, I slipped it around my shoulders, zippered it up to my chin, and pulled the hood over my head. The slight comfort against the cool night air was greatly appreciated.

The dim overhead light cast peculiar shadows as we gave the truck a thorough search. We spoke only to share failure statistics.

The only thing we hadn't searched was what looked like a bundle of camping equipment. "Must be somewhere in there," Sam said.

We both looked at the four-cubed-feet bundle of blue plastic tied up like a Christmas gift with clothesline.

"Seems kind of an inconvenient place to keep your cell phone," I said, thinking out loud.

"Probably dropped it while folding up the equipment. Happens all the time. Help me get these ropes off."

We tried to slip the cords over a corner but the treasure was heavy and rigid, and the ropes were tight and strong.

"I think I saw a knife," Sam said, once she'd broken all ten of her fingernails (mine were already broken) and exhausted our vocabulary of colorful adjectives.

I ducked as first a hammer, then a screwdriver, then some pliers, then more unidentifiable apparatus whizzed past my nose as she tore through the toolbox's contents.

"Here we go." She held up an Exacto knife, the kind used by hobbyists to carve out delicate detail.

I sawed at the ropes, but the going was slow, and I was mildly impatient. Make that maniacally impatient. I gave up on the rope and sliced through the blue plastic, only to find another layer of canvas tarp. I sawed an opening large enough to slip an arm into it, only to find a thick wool blanket. I sliced my way through that and exposed the toe of a running shoe. Hard as I tugged, it wouldn't come out, so I forced my large hand through the tiny hole to feel around.

I squeezed my way up the shoelaces and my hand found a leg. Or at least what felt like a leg. But what would a leg be doing in a plastic-bound bundle in the back of Porter Trawbridge's work truck?

Sliding my hand along the thing that felt like a leg but couldn't be a leg, I discerned fabric. Denim, to be exact. Then a cotton shirt. Not a tent, that's for sure. Was this Porter's dirty laundry? No. Under the fabric was a squishy firmness, like a soft spot on an apple.

Then I felt fingers. The cold fingers of a dead man. No mistaking that.

I yanked my arm out and ran screaming into the night.

Only it was dark, and I couldn't see where I was going. After pinballing off a few trees, I stopped, dropped to the ground and tried to clear the fear away enough to think.

And the most frightening supposition in the world entered my mind. Suppose Sam and I had interrupted Porter Trawbridge's disposal of a dead body. And suppose Porter was hiding in the shadows waiting for us to leave so he could complete his task. And further suppose, now that we'd found the body, he would think it necessary to kill us, too, in order to keep his murderous ways a secret.

I heard Sam scream. The kind of scream emitted when one's throat is being slashed.

RUN was the single thought in my head. I struggled to my feet, but I couldn't move. It was as if my Keds had turned to cement blocks. No matter how much I tried, they were stuck to the ground.

I swiped at the wetness on my cheek. Not sweat wet, but tears wet. I was crying. Tears of fear. I didn't want to die out here in the wilderness, my throat slashed by a cold-blooded killer, my body never to be found.

I stood and cried by the light of the moon, my eyes shut tight, the warm tears sliding down my cheeks and dripping off my chin. I heard the rustling of underbrush then felt a hand on my throat. A warm hand. With strong fingers.

"I swear to gawd, Ellery. If you don't come help me find this cell phone I'm going to choke the life right out of you, sure as you're born." As she spoke, her fingers tightened around my windpipe.

"Dammit, Sam. Don't you ever scare me like that again. I thought you were being murdered." I yanked her hands from my throat and shoved her away.

"Don't you ever leave me to search a dead body alone then. Some friend you are." Sam stood beside me, shaking in her shoe.

She had a point. It had been foolish to run. There existed safety in numbers. And in tools. Armed with a ball peen hammer and hacksaw, we could fight off a killer. Standing here, unarmed, in the dark, we were sitting meerkats.

"So Porter didn't kill you?" I wrapped my arms around Sam and felt her shiver into my embrace. When it came down to it, she was all bluster and no substance. This little woman was ten times more frightened than I was, if that were humanly possible.

Once our tears were exhausted and our sniffles had subsided, we continued to stand still, listening for the sound of Porter coming to get us. All we heard were the sounds of the night.

Eventually I spoke. I couldn't stand here doing nothing any longer. "I'll hike back to civilization and get help," I offered.

"No, don't leave me here alone. I couldn't stand it."

We stood shivering for a few minutes. I pulled Porter's sweatshirt tighter around and tried to work up my courage to go back and face the horrible fact that I'd have to touch a dead body in order to not end up dead myself.

"Who do you think the body is?" Sam asked, her voice as faint as the breeze blowing through the trees.

"Since it's Porter Trawbridge's truck, I'm thinking it's someone he didn't like real well. Did he have any enemies?"

"No. He's a real nice guy. Quiet. Well-respected. Volunteers at the animal shelter every Christmas, since all the other volunteers prefer to be home with their families. He says somebody needs to be with the homeless creatures. He has two cats of his own, Busby and Butch, both pound kitties. But he's a Newbee, so no telling what or who's in his past."

"Do you think he could have killed Reverend Hammersmith?" Somebody needed to try to connect those dots. To my way of thinking, I'd rather have one killer on the loose than two.

"I don't know what to think any more."

More silence.

"Did you find the phone?" I asked, ever so hopeful.

"No. Like you, once I realized what was in the bundle, I ran away."

"We need to get the cell phone if we want to have any hope of getting out of here alive." There, I'd said it. And I'd used the plural pronoun on purpose. Neither of us seemed capable of doing the terrible, horrible, hideously disgusting deed alone. I wasn't all that convinced we could do it together, but we had to try.

Our return to the scene of the body bundle was slow going. Sam had fled without her crutches. Adrenaline can mask pain, but now that the rush was over her ankle must have hurt, judging by the expletives she muttered every time she put even a little bit of weight on it. And it didn't help that the ground was uneven and full of sticks and stones. A snail would have beaten us had we been racing.

We stepped out of the woods and into the clearing. The Explorer waited for us, and with all the doors open and illuminated from the dome light inside it reminded me of a maniacal jack-o-lantern.

"Come on. Let's just get this over with." I marched over to the car, picked Sam's crutches off the ground and tossed them in her direction. I forced all thoughts from my mind as I climbed into the back of the truck and dug through the toolbox until I found a small handsaw. I worked quickly and quietly until the ropes lay around the bundle like a clew of worms.

Sam picked up the hobby knife and climbed into the truck. Her hand shook like an espresso junkie after a morning-long binge, but her movements were deliberate and swift. Two short slices across the top and one long slice down the middle, forming a capital I through the crisscrossed pattern of plastic and duct tape. Then she yanked the plastic back and scrambled out from the track and back to my side. The sound of her knees knocking echoed in the stillness.

"Oh, gawd," she said and shook. We hugged again, each giving and gaining strength from the other. "Your turn." She handed me the knife.

I stared at the bundle, now sliced open like a fresh perch waiting to be gutted. The next layer was thick canvas, the type of oilskin used by professional painters as drop cloths. Should I attempt to cut it open and risk nicking the body underneath? Or should I treat it like a deli sandwich and unwrap it?

I'd decided to unwrap the canvas, because the idea of cutting into a person's flesh, even though he wouldn't feel it, made me queasy.

Before I could talk myself out of it, I reached in and ripped the plastic tarp off, then shoved the dead body around until I had all the edges of the canvas loose.

Suddenly Sam was at my side, scratching and clawing at the blanket until it, too, had been removed.

The man's body, bloated and fleshy after rigor mortis had subsided, was tucked in a fetal position. His profile was visible: prominent nose, dark hooded eyes and about a two day growth of beard. I didn't recognize him as anyone I'd ever seen around Braddocks Beach.

"Oh. My. Gawd," Sam whispered. "It's Porter Trawbridge."

Chapter Twenty-Two

Hard as it was to draw my gaze away from the horrors of a dead body, I forced myself to look around for the cell phone, hoping it was clipped to his belt or had fallen next to his body. But it wasn't anywhere to be seen. That meant one thing. It was tucked in Porter's pocket. "Who's going to get the phone?" I asked.

"No way am I touching him. You do it."

"Not me. You do it."

Sam and I continued in this vein for some time, neither one of us hesitating so much as a nanosecond in our responsive denial for fear that the other would detect weakness and move in for the kill. The conversation reduced itself to a one word Ping-Pong match.

"You."

"You."

"You."

"You."

"Stop," I said before my head exploded. "Let's paper, rock, scissors. On three. One, two, three, shoot." I held out my fist, representing rock.

Sam threw out a half-fist, then flattened it out to paper.

"Paper smothers rock," she said. "I win. You lose. You give Porter the pat down."

I could have argued that she'd cheated but we could have been there all night. I sighed. How hard could this be?

But as I moved closer to the corpse, I found myself

paralyzed by Porter's glassy-eyed stare that seemed to follow my every motion. I looked away, drew a deep breath and managed to drum up more inner courage than I ever knew I possessed. One more deep breath and I grabbed his foot to straighten his leg. As I pulled, the smell of death compounded by the stench of expelled body fluids overpowered me. I kept focused on the task and reached a hand down into the front left pocket of Porter's Levi's. The coldness of his body was the scariest part yet. The entire thing was so surreal, and yet it was very real. Too real. And too, too awful.

My fingers frantically searched for the phone, and finally wrapped around a small rectangular object. In my sweaty, shaky hand I held our ticket out of this wilderness hell.

"Got it." I held the cell phone in my hands. Our only connection to the outside world. Help was only a phone call away.

Sam celebrated by waving her crutches in the air and hopping in circles on one foot.

I opened the phone and prepared to call.

Sam prevented my doing so by putting her hand over the keypad. "They'll think we did it," Sam whispered.

"Huh?"

"Think about it. We'll be the primary suspects. What are the odds of us just happening to travel to this remote area and just happen across a dead guy in his truck? About ten ga-zillion to one."

"I don't care. I'd rather be warm and dry and have three square meals a day in jail than sit here cold and tired and hungry and sharing space with a dead body." I pulled the phone out of her reach and pressed 9-1-1 then TALK. I almost cried when I heard the calm voice of the emergency operator. Quickly I gave the particulars of the situation and detailed the location as best I could.

The operator responded with assurances that help was on

the way, then asked, "Is there a safe place you can go until--"

With an ominous beep, the cell phone's battery died and we were once again isolated with only a dead body for company.

Suddenly I was afraid. Very afraid. No way had Porter driven his own truck out here, killed himself, and then wrapped himself in three layers of protective coating. There was another person out there in the woods. And not just any person. A manically crazed, cold-blooded killer.

I found a head-smashing hammer lying at my feet and an eye-poking screwdriver in my back pocket, although I have no recollection as to how they got there. Thus armed, I stood ready to fight for my life.

"Let's get our stories straight." Sam appeared at my elbow and huddled close. "We received an anonymous tip about a dead body on this property and came out to investigate."

"No good. They'll wonder why we didn't call the police. And probably get a warrant for the phone records only to discover we hadn't made or received a call all afternoon. We need to tell the truth, the whole truth, and nothing but the truth, so help us God."

"No, the truth will land us in jail. Think about it, we just happened to visit the most remote place in the entire state of Ohio and find a dead body? Our fingerprints are all over that truck and the tools and everything. We'll say we didn't call the police when we received the anonymous call because we thought it was a joke."

"No good. If we knew it was a joke, why would we fall for it and haul ourselves all the way out here in the dead of night?" I shivered against the images the word *dead* conjured in my mind. "The truth, Sam. We came out here to look at property and our car died. What makes you think they won't believe that? Wait. Hush. What was that?" I whispered.

Silence.

The seconds ticked away like centuries. The night

remained quiet. The lack of noise was tortuous. Despite the fact the sun hadn't risen and set, I would have sworn we'd stood there for three days.

And then faintly in the distance, a sound, growing louder. Music to my ears...the sound of sirens. Lots of them. Approaching quickly and en masse. Glory, glory, halleluiah, we were saved.

And questioned.

And accused.

And acquitted, since the crime team estimated Porter had been dead for about thirty-six hours, based on body temp and the fact that rigor mortis had begun abating. Lucky us, we had an airtight alibi having spent from Saturday noon until this morning enjoying the hospitality of the Braddocks Beach jail.

"Don't leave town, though," Chief Lewis warned us. "I expect I'll need you to answer a few more questions."

"We can't even get to town to leave it," Sam said, her voice crossing the line to the testy side. "Can someone give us a lift home?"

"Ask Compton."

We found Officer Compton standing in the shadows of his police cruiser, which was in the shadows of the Explorer, which was close enough for us to see the crime technicians working, and if I listened real hard, which I did, I heard them talking.

"Death by strangulation," pronounced a short squatty woman, but said with a niggle of doubt in her voice. She reminded me of Daphne on Scooby Doo, only with more fashionable glasses.

"Good answer," said the tall, skinny woman who carried an aura of authority about her. "But no scratches like you'd get from a coarse rope like nylon. We'll check for fibers, of course, but I'm thinking a soft piece of clothing of some kind. Maybe a sock?"

Of all the years I had washed and worn socks, it had never occurred to me they could be considered a deadly weapon. Scary.

A deep voice from behind startled me. "Hey Miz Greene, Miz Tinsdale."

"Hey, yourself, Titus," Sam greeted the ever faithful tow truck driver. "You here to haul Porter's truck back to town?"

"No, Ma'am. Not to town. I'll be hauling it to Medina. It's a crime scene you know."

"Yes, I know."

"You do?" Titus' eyes darted furtively around the outskirts of our little group, then he leaned in and whispered, "Any idea what happened?"

Sam told him.

Poor Titus. He didn't take the news well. Upon hearing Porter Trawbridge's name, Titus fell to his knees and prayed like I'd never seen anyone pray before. Sam knelt next to him and stroked his arm and soothed his soul. I wrapped my arms around my middle and gave myself a comforting hug. All this death. So senseless. What motive would anyone have for killing a small-town carpenter who spent Christmas day with homeless animals?

And more importantly, was the killer done killing yet?

Chapter Twenty-Three

I rolled into bed about seven a.m. that morning, and was rolled out by Sam at nine. As in a.m., not p.m., which had been my original plan. A whole two hours sleep. And a very restless, disturbed sleep, with the ghost of Porter Trawbridge dancing through my dreams. Needless to say, I was a tad on the grumpy side.

"I can't make the building committee meeting," Sam said as we sat around Aunt Izzy's kitchen table.

"What building committee meeting?" I asked.

"The church is looking at options to build a community center that can hold larger functions than the rec room in the basement. If you don't book the one wedding reception place in town, you have to go to the country club over in Grafton, and that's a long haul home for a lot of people. There's a need, and the money is there, thanks to the tireless efforts of the fundraising committee, and a generous donation from your Aunt. It's taken them six years, but they're just about to their goal."

I washed down another breakfast cookie (aka Pepperidge Farm Mint Milanos) with some room-temperature Diet Coke.

"Since Scott resigned, I'm running RJ's little league practice this morning. I was thinking you should go."

Sam's step-grandson was a really good ball player, and Sam was a really loyal bleacher babe. But I couldn't imagine her as a coach, and I really wasn't in any mood to be her assistant. "I'm not in the mood for a baseball practice. Maybe next time."

"Not to the game, to the meeting. Your name's going to

be on the building, so you should give them your input."

"I'm really tired, Sam."

"I don't know how you can sleep with a killer on the loose."

"I aim to try."

"Let me rephrase. You need to go to the meeting, Ellery."

"Why?"

"Because it will give you the perfect opportunity to check Reverend Hammersmith's schedule for last Thursday. Everyone connected to the church will be at that meeting, including Gayle Somerset, the temporary assistant taking Bing's place while Bing is on her, ah, vacation."

"Vacation" was the polite-society code word for suicide watch at the local mental institution.

"It's the responsibility of the church secretary to record the minutes," Sam continued without benefit of a breath. "So Gayle'll be away from her desk. There won't be a soul around in the business part of the church. With any luck, you'll find out the name of his noon appointment, and we'll have the name of our killer."

"To turn over to the police."

"Absolutely. So you'll go?"

Even though Sam's words indicated I had a choice in the matter, her body language told a different story. I could agree to go now, or I could argue the point and agree to go later. The result would be the same. Sam wasn't going to take no for an answer. "What time and where?"

"Ten o'clock in the church's conference room. It's down in the basement."

"What's the appropriate attire for a church building meeting?" I doubted my current outfit of yoga pants stretched to within a stitch of their lives and *Put Your Pity Party on the Shelf* T-shirt would work.

"Queen Bee Daywear, of course. I called Chiquita and

she should be here any minute."

Chiquita was a local fashion guru who Sam had put on retainer for me. Whenever there was an event for which I had nothing appropriate to wear, one phone call to Chiquita and an entire outfit--complete with foundational garments, shoes, and matching bling--would appear at my door. I had yet to see any of the bills, but I suspected this was the preponderance of the reason Max wanted to discuss my finances. "Thanks," I said.

"And here." Sam pulled her cell phone from her pocket and slid it across the table to me. "I don't imagine yours will work after the dunking it took in the lake yesterday, and we'll need to keep in contact. Ann Marie lost her cell phone privileges for the week so I'll use her I-phone and you can use this one until we can get yours replaced." Sam buzzed off to spread her energy to RJ's little league team, leaving me to dawdle over breakfast and prepare myself for a day of sleuthing (a kinder, gentler word for being nosy.)

Titus hadn't towed my golf cart back to town yet, so my two choices of transportation were the rusty old bicycle or walking. I chose to hoof it, given that it was a nice day and Chiquita, my personal fashionista, had provided me with Easy Spirit pumps that I considered the best thing since sliced baguette. So not only did they feel good, they also looked good and complimented the taupe pants and lightweight shell in a shade that reminded me of a tropical sunset. A jewel-toned silk scarf added a splash of color around my neck and played off a striking pair of enamel earrings. I felt like a million bucks. I just hoped the outfit that seemed tailor made to my unique shape didn't cost anywhere near that much.

Meetings in Braddocks Beach always start at the appointed time. My southern upbringing had me more accustomed to at least thirty minutes of socializing and snacking before getting down to business. To my credit, I arrived at the Braddocks Beach Church of Divine Spiritual Enlightenment

Building Committee Meeting only fifteen minutes past the appointed time.

Not only had the meeting started, so, apparently, had the fighting.

It was quite a scene with raised angry voices, pointing fingers, waving arms, and hand gestures indicating someone was crazy in the head. Within a matter of minutes, the entire crowd of about twenty people were on their feet and shouting. Despite Polly Rutledge's calling for order and banging her gavel until it broke, chaos ensued.

This could be a long meeting, so I looked around for a place to sit. The community room in the church's basement was utilitarian and unimaginative. The painted cinder block walls and linoleum floor were all the same uninspiring shade of dessert sand and served to amplify the cacophony of raised voices. Two rows of metal chairs lined up like squatty soldiers were almost all occupied and faced a U-shaped assemblage of tables with dour-faced committee members holding court behind them.

I noticed raccoon-eyed Buddy Clarke sitting quietly on the sidelines, watching it all with a look of impatience. I scooted into the empty seat next to him and then yelled in his ear, "What's this all about?"

He yelled back, "Some people want the new Tinsdale Community Center to be built on the corner of Boston and Yorktown, but there are size and architectural limitations at that location. And that will require tearing down an historical landmark. Others want to build it on the outskirts of town, where it can be large enough to meet the needs of the community and have a glossy new look to attract the younger generation. But it's about a mile outside of town, and will be a challenge for the older members to get to, especially in colder weather. Few of them drive anymore, preferring to ride their electric chairs to meetings and services."

I nodded, having witnessed the Parade of the Rascals on

Sunday mornings and Wednesday evenings. Both arguments had merit, but nothing was going to be solved by shouting. I sat back and watched a little longer. Neither side seemed to be gaining any ground. I leaned toward Buddy and yelled again. "You don't seem to have an opinion, so why are you here?"

"I drew up the plans and cost estimates for both options. I'm just waiting for the decision so I can move forward with the construction bidding."

I settled back again and noticed two easels set up at the far corner of the room. My eyesight's not what it used to be, but the difference between the two was like a time warp that spanned two centuries. The first rendering, a four-story structure with tall skinny windows separated by a few white scalloped clapboards and a steep red-shingled roof topped with a crow's nest, reminded me of the Hotel Del in Coronado, California. It emitted a romantic aura that brought back a lot of memories of a great honeymoon. I sighed. The other, also a four story structure, was the stuff of which urban skylines are made. Constructed entirely of green glass and steel, it was clean, crisp, contemporary, and sterile. It made me want to throw stones at it.

I leaned toward Buddy and yelled again, "Did Reverend Hammersmith have a preference?"

Buddy shook his head.

That surprised me. I couldn't imagine the old-fashioned reverend swooshing around in that new-fangled monstrosity. "Is there any sort of compromise?"

"Nothing to make everyone happy."

The police arrived and did their best to sort out the melee.

My cell phone buzzed in my pocket, so I slipped out of the room to answer it. "Hello Sam."

"Is the meeting over?" she asked.

"The fighting's over. The meeting's just starting."

"You'd better tap into that file while everyone is

otherwise occupied. You might not get another chance. *Run, Dalton! Ruuuuunnnnn.*" I had to pull my phone away from my ear before Sam's shouts deafened me. "Gotta go. Problems on the field. Call me when you find something. *There's no crying in baseball, Spencer. Now pick up your glove and get back out there. Carter, you take first--*"

I snapped my phone shut, listened for a few moments to the raised but civil voices inside the meeting room, then tiptoed down the linoleum and painted cinder block passage decorated with Sunday school artwork, up the stairs and along the carpeted and paneled vestibule. I turned left down the passageway that led to Bing's office, which in turn led to Reverend Hammersmith's office, now crisscrossed in yellow Crime Scene tape.

An image flashed in my head of the reverend lying with his head on his desk, and his chicken salad sandwich splattered in what Sam described as Ketchup. Being this close to where he died erased my arm's length approach to our investigation. Now it seemed real. A real murder. A real killer. And a real need to see his calendar in hopes of finding the person who has no regard for human life.

I approached Bing's desk. The good Lord willing, I'd find the calendar somewhere in Bing's territory and not inside the reverend's bloody inner sanctum. I wasn't sure I'd be able to go in there.

I sat in Bing's chair, typical secretary style with a seat and a back (no arms) on wheels and bellied up to the workstation. I tapped into her Dell. Access was password protected. No luck finding an obtuse string of letters and numbers which might gain me access so I crossed my fingers and hoped the reverend was like me, a hard-copy kind of guy.

I rolled myself over to the line of two-drawer file cabinets behind the workstation. The chair scratched against the carpet protector and squeaked under the duress of my shifting weight. I stopped and froze. Silence descended again. No sounds of running footsteps to check out the source of the noise. After a few heartbeats of silence, I resumed my sneaky search.

Bing deserved a gold star for file maintenance, as everything was neatly labeled and in logical order. I soon found one marked "Calendars, Monthly" right between "Building Fund" and "Capital Improvements". Inside were printouts of weekly calendars and on top was the reverend's schedule for last week.

Only two names appeared on the block for Thursday, July 14th; a ten-thirty appointment with Porter Trawbridge, (I murmured "Peace be with him" when I saw the name) and a two p.m. meeting with Janet Staunton ("Peace be with her"). The entire rest of the afternoon was blocked out for PERSONAL.

How odd was it that all of those three people ended up dead?

So who had Reverend Hammersmith been expecting at noon? Either it had been a last minute arrangement that didn't make it to his schedule, or it was with someone he didn't want his secretary to know about.

But since when does the Grim Reaper make an appointment?

Chapter Twenty-Four

As I sat there contemplating death's recent visit to Reverend Hammersmith's office, it felt as if a cold, ghostly vapor was replacing my hot, human blood. I have never believed in ghosts, but I have never *not* believed in them either. Could the restless spirit of Reverend John Thomas Hammersmith, murdered not more than ten feet from where I sat, be taking up residence in my body?

Or could all this poking my nose into places my nose had no business being poked be playing havoc with my nerves? I can be such a Nervous Nelly.

I'd completed my tasking so I slipped the folder back into its slot where I'd found it. Without any conscious effort on my part at all, the Building Fund file came out when I withdrew my hand from the drawer. As I placed it on top of the file cabinet, it just happened to fall open, and my eyes just happened to scan the column of numbers. It seems as if I'd caught a bad case of Sam's "nosy" bug.

The fund was well-funded. A quick flip to the most recent bank statement showed that it was also thoroughly-drained. Only a few hundred thousand dollars remained from an original reserve of over two million, and they hadn't even broken ground yet. But the bottom line on the Construction Report showed a hefty balance of funds available. What was up with that?

"Nancy Drew, I presume?" a deep voice said from behind me.

I jumped six feet out of my chair, sending it clattering across the plastic carpet protector and slamming into Bing's desk. I looked over my shoulder to find Chief Lewis staring at me, his thumbs tucked in his utility belt as he rocked back on his heels. Judging by his narrowed eyes and stern mouth, he was not at all happy to see me.

The feeling was mutual.

"Care to share your finding?"

"Hmmm? What? Findings? I don't know what you're talking about." I turned to face him, putting on my innocent act to the best of my ability. My performance wouldn't garner me an Emmy nomination. Not even close.

Chief Lewis dipped his head and his gaze towards the opened file.

"Oh, this?" I said, my voice a half-octave higher than it usually was, revealing to all in hearing range just how discomposed I was at the moment. So discomposed that I couldn't even come up with a teensy weensy fib, let alone a bold-faced lie. It seems the truth was my best--and only--option. "This is the Building Fund file, for the new community center. They're discussing it downstairs right now."

"I'm aware of the meeting. And I'm wondering why you're up here and not down there yourself."

"Me? Oh, well." My brain was spinning like a hamster on an exercise wheel, getting nowhere fast.

"I think you and I need to have a little chat. Sit." He motioned to the chair that had spun away from me.

I reached out and pulled it towards me and sat. I can be very obedient, especially when the person giving orders has a gun.

"You and Mrs. Greene have been asking a lot of questions. I want to know what answers you've got."

"None. No answers." Dang. He'd just tricked me into admitting we'd been asking questions. Chief Lewis was good.

"I didn't fall off the turnip truck yesterday, Ms. Tinsdale.

All those damn shows on TV have every Tom, Rick and Carrie wanting to play police detective, and you two are the worst I've seen yet. Not that anything you've learned by your methods would be admissible in a court of law, but I need to know where your information is taking you."

"Nowhere."

Chief Lewis' mouth drew into a tight, thin line. "Need I remind you that the two of you have been the first on the scene when all three bodies were found? Reverend Hammersmith." He began ticking names off on his fingers. "Janet Staunton and Porter Trawbridge. I have enough evidence to hold you on suspicion of murder. You could be locked up for days. Weeks, even."

"And need I remind you I have enough friends in high places to have me released within hours." That wasn't a bluff. Between Max and George Greene, not to mention the weight the Tinsdale name carried locally, I felt confident in that statement.

Chief Lewis began pacing back and forth in front of Bing's desk like a lion at the zoo. Slow, powerful movements with eyes staring beyond the bars as if saying *I could eat you if I wanted to. I just choose not to right now.*

Nerve-wracking, to say the least.

"Okay, how's this. How about we play a little Tit for Tat. Know what that is?"

I nodded. "Otherwise known in the political world as 'You scratch my back I'll scratch yours.'"

"Very good, Ms. Tinsdale."

"You go first," I said, being the gracious Queen Bee that I am. And also fearing if I went first that I wouldn't get my back scratched. Ever.

"All right. How's this?" He stopped right in front of Bing's desk, leaned over and placed his meaty paws so that they straddled an overstuffed pencil cup. "As you are probably well aware, Porter Trawbridge held a winning lottery ticket worth seven-point-nine million dollars. You may not know that said lottery ticket is missing. We believe that may have been why he was killed. Your turn."

"Okay," I said, refusing to be intimidated by his position of superiority as he hovered above me. "How's this? Porter locked his ticket in a safety deposit box."

"No, he didn't. There is no deposit box registered in his name in any bank in town."

Hmmm. Now that was interesting.

"Lottery tickets are bearer instruments," Chief Lewis continued. "Whoever holds that ticket is gonna come into a whole lotta money. Might even be enough to kill for." He stood up. "Your turn."

If nothing else, I play fair. So I told him what I'd just learned about the building fund. "Here," I said, reaching behind me for the file and handing it to him. "There's the money trail. And Porter Trawbridge had an appointment with Reverend Hammersmith two hours before he was killed. Janet Staunton two hours after. I'll let you connect the dots. That's why they pay you the big bucks."

I got out of my chair and exited the office with confidence and sass, and an extra splash of aplomb. Move over Hillary Swank. There's a new actress in town.

Chapter Twenty-Five

No sooner had I changed out of my Queen Bee Daywear and into my Plain Old Me Loungewear (old leather flip flops, baggy cargo shorts, old and stained T-shirt that said A Balanced Diet Is a Cookie in Each Hand) than Sam banged through the kitchen door.

I'd never seen her dressed in anything that didn't bear a designer label, and it took me a moment to wrap my head around this casual version of Sam. This morning she sported white cotton shorts and a yellow and black Killer Bees uniform shirt. She'd pulled her usual not-a-curl-out-of-place hair into a ponytail and pulled the ponytail through the back opening of the cap. Her single Ked shoe was as brilliantly white as the moment it had come out of the box. How did she manage to stay so clean? More importantly, is it something she could teach me?

"Did you find out who had the noon appointment?" she asked.

"No noon appointment on the reverend's calendar."

"So we've got nothing." She collapsed into a kitchen chair.

"No, we've got something. A great big whale-sized something."

"Do tell."

I settled into the seat across from her, popped open a Snapple and told her about Porter's missing lottery ticket.

"How's that good news? I don't know a single person that couldn't use seven-point-nine million dollars. That doesn't narrow down our list of suspects at all."

"Add it to this. Porter Trawbridge had a ten o'clock appointment with Reverend Hammersmith."

"So?"

"So, Porter's in construction, right?"

"Yup. He was on the payroll for the church, handling the business end of construction projects. Mostly authorizing expenses and paying bills. I'm sure he'd have overseen the community center construction."

"Not if there wasn't any money to build it."

"What?"

I filled Sam in on what I found, or more accurately what I hadn't found, in the building fund file. For the first time in the five weeks I'd known her, Sam was speechless. Body still, mouth open, eyes blinking speechless.

"Did anyone actually see Porter's winning ticket?" I asked.

"What are you getting at?"

"I'm questioning its existence. Try this theory on for size. If Porter had skimmed a huge chunk of money from the fund—"

Sam waved her arms in the air to stop me. "You didn't know Porter. He was as honest as the day is long."

"What do you base that on? He's a Newbee."

"But he wouldn't have lasted a month in this town if he practices dishonest business dealings—"

"Just hear me out here. If Porter had skimmed money, and then claimed he won the Classic Lotto, he could shake off the dust of this one stoplight town and head for the tropics and nobody would even question how he could afford to do so on his carpenter's salary. It's the perfect cover. Especially if no one ever suspected him of skimming."

I could see the cogs in Sam's brain starting to move. "He isn't from around here. In fact, I don't know anything about his life before he moved here three years ago."

"Say Reverend Hammersmith found out about the missing money and confronted Porter—"

"So Porter splattered the reverend's brain all over his lunch in order to cover the theft."

Leave it to Sam to express things so eloquently. "I'm just saying…" I shrugged my shoulders and held my hands out, palms up.

"Then why was Porter killed?"

"As Chief Lewis hinted at, a lottery ticket is a bearer instrument. If somebody thought Porter had it, it might be worth killing for. Only Porter never had a ticket."

"Come on," Sam said, rethreading her pony tail through her ball cap. "We're going to Tinky's."

No need to ask me twice. It was lunchtime, and it being Monday and all, Tinky's world famous Reuben with homemade thousand-island dressing would be the special.

I snagged a sweatshirt off the hook by the back door and shrugged it on. While Sam's casual attire was within the summer-tourist-casual dress code of Tinky's, my Plain Old Me Loungewear had a big greasy spot, a reminder of gravies past, right in the center. Queen Bees should never be seen in public in stained clothing. That lesson had been drummed into my head my first week of training. Fortunately the sweatshirt was black so didn't clash with my outfit, and was lightweight, which was important since the temperature today was supposed to flirt with 80 degrees. Queen Bees aren't supposed to sweat, either.

As always during the summer outside of Tinky's, the line of people stretched half a block long. That didn't faze Sam. She maneuvered her crutches past the gaggle of tourists and through the front door, acting as if she were a Mafia Don entering an Italian Restaurant. I tagged along as if I were the heat-packing bodyguard.

Every table was occupied, but one four-topper had only one occupant. Sam bee-lined it that way. It was our lucky day.

The lone diner was Polly Rutledge, the head of the Church of Divine Spiritual Enlightenment building project and wife of the town's duly elected coroner.

Polly must have worked up quite an appetite wielding the gavel at the building committee meeting, because she was tucking into a Reuben sandwich, with sauerkraut, dressing and pastrami oozing out over the edge of the toasted rye bread. The way she stuffed that food in her face you'd a thunk she hadn't eaten in a week.

I used the back of my hand to wipe off the saliva seeping out of the corner of my mouth. Queen Bees don't drool, either.

"Morning, Polliwog," Sam said and smiled. She pulled out the chair across from Polly and sat down. "Mind if we join you?"

Polly Rutledge didn't look anywhere near as intimidating with a fork in her hand instead of a gavel. Oh sure, she was still sporting her navy pinstripe power suit and her halo of Miss Clairol Number 5R hair still showed evidence of careful grooming, but we caught her using her French-tipped pinky to push a stray bit of sauerkraut into her over stuffed mouth. She paused mid-push and gave us a nod. While her head indicated her permission to join the table, her eyes said, "Get lost!"

"How did the meeting go this morning?" Sam asked.

Polly swallowed, then answered, "As well as can be expected."

"Meaning?"

"There are some very strong opinions on either side of the issue. We've adjourned until more information is forthcoming."

"You mean more information about how the building fund is practically gone?" Sam asked.

I saw it, a brief flicker of disbelief on Polly's face, followed by confusion, then dismissal. "I don't know where you got that information. The building fund is fine. I audited the books last month. In fact, it's about to become a whole lot bigger. So much so that we might be able to build both centers."

"What do you mean?" Sam asked.

"Nothing. I shouldn't have said anything."

"Polly, this information could be critical to finding out who is sneaking through the streets of Braddocks Beach and killing people."

"Sam, it's not my place to say anything. You'll find out when the will is probated, just like everyone else. Oops."

"What? Whose will? Porter's? Reverend Hammersmith's? Janet Staunton's? Or did No-No Nanette finally kick the bucket?"

I leaned into the conversation and asked, "Who's No-No Nanette?"

"She's a very wealthy woman who moved to Palm Springs years ago," Sam explained to me. "But she kept Max on as her estate attorney, and word on the street is that the Church of Divine Spiritual Enlightenment will be remembered fondly in her will. But No-No is too ornery to ever die."

I sat back in my chair, happy to return to my role as spectator to the conversation and noodling around the question as to how a woman earned the nickname No-No.

Polly pushed her half-eaten lunch away and pulled her Vera Wang purse onto her lap. She was fiddling for money, and I suspected about to make a run for it. Sam must have realized that too, because she used her elbows to pull her upper body across the table until her chin nearly dipped into a filled-to-the-brim glass of icy cola.

"Who left a bundle to the church?" Sam asked, her steely gaze making threats that scared the beejeezus out of me. And I wasn't even on the receiving end of the look.

Polly pushed away from Sam, and in the process shoved her plate of food forward. A French fry drenched in ketchup flipped off the plate and clung to Sam's yellow Killer Bees jersey. Uh oh.

Sam didn't move. Not to wipe off the ketchup. Not to push the stray curl out of her eye. Not even to acknowledge the "Hey Mrs. Greene" from a young girl walking by the table. Never before had I seen Sam ignore a friendly salutation. Never. This was serious.

Sam stared at Polly, and when she spoke, it was in a light, conversational tone, which served to make the threat more threatening. "If you don't give me an answer within the next five seconds, I will make sure Ozzy rides the pine pony for the rest of the season."

Ozzy Rutledge was Polly and Bernard's ten-year-old grandson. He was the ace pitcher for the Killer Bees team. The team was four games away from winning the pennant. If Ozzy was benched, the team could lose. Make that would lose. Timmy, the backup, only managed to throw one strike every fifteen pitches or so, and the other teams all knew it.

Was Sam willing to risk her step-grandson's victory over this bit of information, or was this an idle threat? I wondered.

Polly seemed to be wondering the same thing. She lowered her brow and peered at Sam through narrowed eyes.

Sam's husband George sponsored the team. We all knew Sam could make good on the threat.

Polly's grandson had talent, and could play on any team in the town.

Silence spread across the restaurant as if someone had dimmed the lights in a theater. People stopped chattering, forks stopped clattering, and the grease stopped splattering. Even the music had gone to static. All eyes were trained on my tablemates.

The standoff at the OK Corral didn't have half the tension that existed between these two women. I pushed my chair away, sensing a rumble in the offing. Blood was rarely drawn in polite Braddocks Beach society, but a civilized food fight had been known to break out when circumstances warranted.

Polly's nostrils flared like a race horse coming down the home stretch.

Sam's blond eyebrows melded in the middle like one big fuzzy worm.

Both maintained deep, slow breathing.

The drip of a coffee maker ticked away the seconds.

Some joker at the next table whistled the High Chaparral tune.

As silence soaked up the mournful notes, Polly blinked.

Chapter Twenty-Six

At Polly's sign of weakness, Sam moved in for the kill. She pushed herself further across the table until their eyelashes touched. She spoke in a voice so low I had to lean in until my eyelashes were in on the action, too.

"I'll make sure Ozzy never plays little league in this town again," Sam threatened.

"Not here." Polly rose from her seat, stuffed a salad-dressing-stained napkin under her plate and stomped out of Tinky's.

Sam's raised voice carried across the hushed room. "Laverne, put that on Ms. Tinsdale's tab, please. And add in a generous tip for your troubles." She stood, smoothed out the creases in her shorts, adjusted the neckline on her stained Killer Bees jersey then tore out of the restaurant as if she were competing for a gold medal in the Olympics. She'd have won one, too, had she not been on crutches.

Not one to be left behind, I waddled to catch up.

I'm sure people wondered where a woman in a business suit, a baseball coach in a yellow jersey and on crutches, and a large woman wearing shorts and a sweatshirt on a 90-degree day were heading. I was wondering myself. I gotta give Polly credit; even in her heels she set a pretty good pace. And Sam, challenged as she was with the bum ankle, kept up. Even though I had two good legs and comfortable shoes, I lagged a few paces behind on account of I was in terrible—make that pathetic—physical shape.

All of us were winded when we finally reached our

destination and plopped into the Adirondack rockers on Polly's front porch at her historic home on Quebec Street. Of the three of us, I was breathing the hardest, but Polly and Sam were winded as well.

As we sat and caught our breath, Sam pulled a Tide to Go stick out of her cleavage and within a few seconds had erased all traces of the ketchup stain on her Killer Bees jersey.

So one secret of the universe was revealed…Sam carried concealed cleaning products in order to maintain that fresh-from-the-dry-cleaner-bag look. Who'd a thunk…

"Okay," Sam said, replacing the lid and returning the laundry stick to her pocket. "Start talking, Polliwog. Who died and left a bundle to the church?"

Polly seemed to be choosing her words very carefully. "I'll tell you what I know. But this is not, and I repeat *not*, to be broadcast over a microphone at the next press conference."

Sam had the good grace to look sheepish at the reference to her blabbing the Scott/Bing affair.

"Swear?" Polly said.

Sam put her right hand over her heart and held her left hand in the air. "On my Granny Annie's grave. Ellery, you swear, too."

"I swear."

"On your Aunt Izzy's grave," Sam prompted.

"On Aunt Izzy's grave," I said.

Polly glanced around, then began to speak. "Porter Trawbridge told me a few weeks ago that he named the church as his primary beneficiary in his new will. Granted, he didn't have much before he won the lottery, but Max confirmed the proceeds of the winning ticket would be part of Porter's estate and would come to the church. Said it's the first place he's felt at home in his whole life. Max is his executor, so when he gets back he'll have access to the safety deposit box and the ticket can be cashed in for seven point nine million dollars." Polly sat back and fanned her glowing face with her hand.

"Except there is no safety deposit box that contains a ticket." Oops, had I said that out loud?

Two heads turned to look in my direction. One showed patent disbelief, the other, slow-simmering anger.

"Ellery," Sam said, the exasperation evidenced in her voice.

"What? Chief Lewis didn't tell me not to tell anyone."

A look of concern spread across Polly's face. "If it's not locked up, then where can it be?"

"Ellery and I have reason to believe that the ticket never existed. That Porter made that story up to cover his embezzlement from the building fund."

"Oh no, the lottery ticket existed all right. He was eating a cinnamon bun at Reba's and reading the Plain Dealer when he saw the numbers. He showed everyone who was in the Pie-ery."

And thus our list of potential suspects was shortened to a few early morning cinnamon bun eaters.

"Who all was there?" Sam asked. Great minds do think alike.

"I wasn't there myself," Polly said. "But you can ask Buddy Clarke. Word coming down the gossip vine is he's the one who suggested Porter lock it up in a safety deposit box, and they marched down to the bank together."

"Thanks, Polly. That helps a lot. We'll stop by Buddy's office then." Sam and I got up from our seats. "Oh, and I suspect Ozzy will be starting pitcher tomorrow night against the Blazers."

"You might want to check that building fund," I said as I walked past Polly. "I'm pretty sure you'll find it almost empty. It might have happened in the past few weeks." I was getting pretty good at this Tit for Tat business.

Sam and I clattered down the front porch steps and took off at a trot (me) and a skip (Sam and her crutches) towards Buddy Clarke's house, which was two blocks over on Princeton

Street.

We used the time to defrag our clues.

"Let's do a timeline," Sam said. "Porter Trawbridge, who had won the lottery a week ago Monday, had a meeting with Reverend Hammersmith at ten a.m. last Thursday morning. Reverend Hammersmith was killed two hours later. Janet Staunton was supposed to meet Reverend Hammersmith at two. She ended up dead around five that day. Porter was killed on Saturday afternoon."

"Do we know yet if Janet was killed or died of natural causes?"

"Easy enough to find out." Sam stopped and pulled her granddaughter's shiny new cell phone out of her pocket and made a call. "Polly," Sam said into her phone. "One more question. Did Bernard happen to say if Janet Staunton's death was suspicious or if she died of natural causes? Umhmm. Really. A deal? What kind of deal. I don't know. I'll ask her and call you right back." Sam disconnected and turned to me. "Polly says she'll tell us if you'll give her your Aunt Izzy's secret recipe for Chocolate Chip Cookies."

"What secret recipe?"

"A recipe for the hands-down best chocolate chip cookies on earth. It was Mizizzy's trademark dish, what she brought to every potluck. Nobody could ever duplicate it quite right. Your aunt guarded that secret the way Coca Cola keeps a lid on their ingredients. Polly wants to bake the cookies and sell them warm from the oven. Unless you intend to take that over as your signature dish."

"I don't bake," I reminded her. "I'm a really good eater, though."

"Which means you won't be needing your Aunt Izzy's recipe."

"Maybe I could sell it to the highest bidder?" That could be the answer to my financial quagmire.

"Queen Bees don't make money off their dead relative's secret recipes."

I wondered if that were in the Queen Bee handbook or if Sam was making that up. But there were still ways to make a sweet deal. "Tell Polly I'll give her the recipe in exchange for a dozen fresh from the oven cookies every week for the next two years."

Sam took out her cell phone, made the call and sealed the deal. "Thanks, Polly." She hung up, re-holstered her cell phone and we started walking again. "Polly said Bernard said Janet died of a stroke. No indication of foul play whatsoever, so not part of this whole murderous mess, just one of those eerie coincidences."

Which makes one wonder; are Reverend Hammersmith's and Porter Trawbridge's murders connected? Or just one of those eerie coincidences, too?

Chapter Twenty-Seven

Buddy Clarke had converted his garage into an office for his architectural business, so we trotted and skipped right past the front door and headed down the recently seal-coated driveway. A nicely tended border garden hugged the path that led around to a side door. Buddy either had a green thumb, or paid someone handsomely who did.

Since it was a place of business and the sign on the door said, "Come On In," we did just that.

Buddy's office was a study in orderly chaos. Two work stations made of a sheet of plywood perched atop sawhorses were stacked with mountains of files, as was just about every available square inch of floor space. I wondered if the row of a dozen or so filing cabinets were full of even more files, or lined up along the wall just for show, to add a splash of color to the otherwise drab office space. A two-foot wide path through the clutter led to each of the work spaces and to a portable partition separating off the back of the garage.

"I hope that's my lunch," Buddy called from behind a partition. "I'm about to die from starvation here."

"Sorry, Buddy. It's only Ellery and me," Sam called back.

Buddy stepped out to the main space to greet us, wiping orange Cheetos dust from his hands onto his khaki pants before extending one for us to shake.

"Ms. Tinsdale and Mrs. Greene. To what do I owe this honor?" Buddy's eyes, still with the shadowy remnants of our collision a few days ago, were smiling when he first saw me, then darkened into unhappy slivers. "Nice sweatshirt," he said.

I looked down at the sweatshirt I'd snagged from the hook and realized it was the one I'd found in the back of Porter's truck. The one declaring alliance to The Ohio State Buckeyes. I'd hung it by the back door so that I could drop it off to his heirs, not realizing at the time that he didn't have any.

"Buddy is a University of Michigan grad," Sam said.

"True blue and gold," he crowed.

The rivalry between Ohio State and Michigan was legendary.

"What can I do for you ladies?" he asked, not seeming to hold the Buckeyes sweatshirt against me.

"We have a few questions for you." Sam leaned back against one of the many file cabinets that lined the wall.

For lack of chairs, I did the same. I needed to catch my breath.

"Who all was in Reba's when Porter found out he'd won the lottery?"

Buddy seemed confused at the question for a moment then looked up at the fluorescent ceiling lights as he seemed to search his memory for that morning. Eventually he rattled off a list of a dozen or so names that meant absolutely nothing to me. I hoped Sam was taking mental notes.

"Did you actually have eyes on the winning ticket?" Sam asked.

"Sure did. Even held it in my hands for about twenty seconds. Porter'd played the numbers he'd gotten from a fortune cookie the day before. I can still remember them. Six, eleven, thirteen, twenty-two, thirty-three and forty-six. We must have repeated them back to each other a dozen times. I doubt I'll ever forget that moment."

So much for my fake-winning-the-lottery theory.

"Then you accompanied him to the bank?" Sam asked.

"Yep. It was either that or drive to the office supply store in Medina to get a fireproof safe to bury it in the backyard. The bank seemed safer and more expedient."

"Which bank did you use?"

"Chase."

"Did you go inside with him?" Sam asked.

"No, I waited outside."

"So, you didn't actually see him put the ticket in a box?"

"No, but why would he hold on to that? It wasn't safe."

Obviously not.

"What's it like holding a piece of paper worth a fortune?" I asked.

"Words cannot explain." He smiled.

"Then what did you do?" Sam asked.

"We came over to my house and celebrated with a bottle of twelve-year-old Scotch and came up with some ideas on how to spend all that money. I think a microbrewery was in his immediate plans."

"Guess there won't be any Trawbridge Ale on tap in Braddocks Beach anytime soon." Sam pushed herself away from the file cabinets and headed for the door. "Thanks for your time, Buddy."

Sam and I retraced our steps back to town at a pace more in keeping with the sultry summer day. "We'll stop by Uncle Swifty's house first. The Monday Morning Marauders Bridge Club will be in full swing. Despite the name, they play all day. Three of the people Buddy mentioned play in that club."

"Wait, since when did it become our responsibility to find Porter's killer? I only signed on to help find Reverend Hammersmith's killer."

"Can you honestly say the two are not related?"

"No."

"Well then, let's just do everything in our power to make Braddocks Beach safe again, shall we?"

I suppose that would be the Queen Bee thing to do. It's

not like I had any big plans for the day, except to eat lunch and take a siesta in the hammock, which were pretty important. But since I'd signed on with Sam, I knew it best to finish the task and then, and only then, would we rest.

We spent the rest of the afternoon tracking down people who'd been in Reba's the morning that Porter had discovered he'd hit the big numbers. All were locals. All were over the age of seventy-five. None were killers, unless they bored someone to death with their stories of the good old days. By the time we'd finished talking to everyone, I wanted to shove knitting needles into my eardrums. Seriously, had there been a pair of size tens available, I would have.

Sam pulled out her cell phone and checked the time. "Where has this day gone? Now we've missed banking hours." She headed for the nearest bench in Tinsdale Park and collapsed, body stretched out from one end of the bench to the other with her head lolling back over the arm rest. I realized what a toll an entire day racing back and forth across town on crutches had taken when her eyes drifted shut.

I pushed her feet to the ground then slumped down in the vacant space. I felt every bit as tired as Sam looked. "Can't you use the ATM?"

"I don't need to make a withdrawal. I wanted to talk to Lawson Smith, the branch manager at Chase Bank, to find out why Buddy said Porter had locked up his ticket, yet Chief Lewis didn't find a box in Porter's name. Something's not adding up here."

"Could Porter have used a different name?"

"No, you have to have ID when you access a box."

"I was able to get into my parent's box."

"Interesting. You must have been on the access list. I guess Porter could have had some connection to the town I don't know about, but what are the odds of that?"

"What, that he has connections or that you don't know

about them?"

Sam chuckled and sat up straight. "Both are infinitesimal, but worth considering."

Why hadn't I kept my big mouth shut?

"A sister or an ex-wife or someone that included him on their access to a safety deposit box," Sam said, running with the idea. "It never occurred to me to ask him what, or who, brought him to Braddocks Beach three years ago. There has to be some connection."

"Porter Trawbridge might not even be his real name." I sat up straighter. Sam's enthusiasm was always contagious. Too bad there wasn't an inoculation for it. "Maybe he's in the witness protection program or running from the mob or skipping out on child support payments so was using a different identity here in Braddocks Beach. Then he could have opened a safety deposit box under his real name but Chief Lewis would have only checked under the name Porter Trawbridge."

"I do believe you're starting to think like a criminal, Ellery."

I'm sure Sam meant that as a compliment.

Chapter Twenty-Eight

"So, now what?" Okay, that was a stupid question to ask Sam, because the answer was bound to be something other than food or rest, which is all I really wanted after an inadequate amount of either the past four and a half days.

Sam pulled out Ann Marie's iPhone and started typing. "Let's make a list of questions we need to answer."

"The only question I need an answer to is who killed Reverend Hammersmith and Porter Trawbridge."

"No need to be snarky, El."

"No need to call me El, Sam." I'd made it very clear on our first meeting that I didn't like my name shortened. El was not a name, merely a letter in the alphabet, and Ellie brought back too many bad memories of third grade boys discovering it rhymed with Smelly.

"My apologies. I think the stress is taking its toll on both of us. I can't help but think we're getting close. Very close. So let's push this through to the end."

There goes Sam channeling her inner cheerleader again.

"We need to find out about Porter's life before Braddocks Beach." She typed something into the cell phone. "And we need to find out from Lawson over at Chase Bank if Porter Trawbridge ever went into the safety deposit box area, and if so, under what name." Type, type, type. "Do you remember the name of the bank on the bank statement you saw in the building fund file?"

"It might have been Chase. But then it could have been B

of BB." Bank of Braddocks Beach was the one preferred by Oldbees, while Chase was the choice of the Newbees. B of BB was the logical choice for the church to use, but I don't think it was their logo on the top of the bank statement page. "I honestly don't remember."

"No worries. I've got connections to both. We need to confirm if the building fund really had been depleted or if maybe just transferred to a higher yielding money market account or something. And if there had been withdrawals, then who had made them."

"We still haven't heard who delivered Reverend Hammersmith's lunch on Thursday." The chicken salad on whole wheat with, perhaps, a side order of a fatal bullet.

"Glad you remembered that. I got so wrapped up with Porter's body I'd completely forgotten about that. So we need to talk to Libby." Type, type, type. Stop. She laid the cell phone in her lap and stretched out her thumbs. "Here's what I'm thinking. I'll send out a few emails to the two banking people I know, then we'll swing by Porter's neighborhood and ask around, see if anyone knew anything about his life prior to moving to Braddocks Beach. Then we'll call Tinky's and have dinner delivered by Libby, and we'll meet at your house. After dinner we'll look around in your basement for the secret cookie recipe for Polly. Then we'll call it a night."

"Why the basement?"

Sam sat uncharacteristically silent next to me.

"Sam, why would we need to search the basement for Aunt Izzy's recipe? Why not her stack of cookbooks or file cabinets or computer records?"

"Because I've already searched all those places and didn't find it."

"How long have you been searching Aunt Izzy's house?"

"From when she died until you showed up, all right? It's a very important piece of Braddocks Beach history and I wanted to make sure it was preserved. But then you moved in and I didn't think it right for me to go snooping around your house."

Glad to hear she had some standards.

"Now let's get to work."

I sat and noodled around in my mind what heart-attack-in-a-box I would order for dinner while Sam sent off a few emails requesting information from her banker friends in high places. Whether she used kindly worded requests or thinly veiled threats of blackmail, I didn't want to know.

"Let's roll," Sam said. "I want to swing by Porter's house and take a peek at what's in his mailbox. Maybe this will be as easy as finding a letter addressed alter persona."

Our sleuthing experience had shown that nothing was ever as easy as we expect.

We hauled ourselves off the park bench—Sam much more gracefully than I—and headed north then east to Porter's house, an old garage that had been transformed into a cute-as-a-bug's-ear cottage. Instead of knocking on any of the neighbor's doors as I thought was the plan, Sam headed straight for Porter's red front door, which had a slot in it for the mail to be deposited right into his living room. No way of casually flipping through it.

Sam raised her hand and rapped her knuckles on the thick oak door.

"You don't expect anyone to be at home, do you?" I asked, my question tinged with a wee bit of snarkiness.

"Nope. Just common courtesy." She rapped again, and this time the door swung open just a teeny tiny bit.

We waited. The door didn't open further. Nor did anyone greet us with a welcoming "Hello." Nor was it slammed shut in our faces.

"That's odd," Sam said, inching closer. She reached out the tip of her crutch and nudged the door ever so gently. This time it swung open and we had a view of Porter's living room, in all its devastated glory.

"What the h-e-double-hockey-sticks…" Sam took two steps into the room and stopped, her head moving from left to right then right to left. "Ellery, call the police."

Something must be terribly amiss if Sam was willing to involve the police. "What's wrong?" Oh lord; she hadn't stumbled on another dead body, had she? What if there was blood splattered on the wall or puddling on the carpet? I couldn't take that, didn't want to see that, so I backed away from the door and kept backing up until I reached the sidewalk. I fished Sam's cell phone out of my pocket and called nine-one-one.

At the sound of sirens, Sam emerged from the house, moving at a really good clip. She used her crutch to point in the direction of our homes then took off in that direction. I followed, and we both managed to sneak down the back alley and be gone from the scene before the police arrived.

I caught up with her and asked, "Who's dead now?"

"What do you mean, 'Who's dead?' Nobody's dead."

"The mess, the way you told me to call nine-one-one I just assumed, well, ah…"

"You assumed wrong. I needed you to call the police because somebody had tossed Porter's place. Like you see on TV when somebody's looking for drugs or something. Not a pillow went un-slashed or a picture frame un-smashed. What a mess."

"So why are we leaving?"

"Because we have better things to do than stand around and answer a lot of questions. Besides, I found out what we needed to know."

"Which is?"

"As you suspected, Porter Trawbridge was not his real name."

"So, who is he?" Really, since when was it so hard to get Sam to talk?

"According to his files—"

"You went through his personal files?"

"They were lying all over the floor. I can't tell my eyes not to read something, can I?"

Still, it didn't seem right.

"His name is Augustus Paul Davidson the fourth."

"So?"

"Remember me mentioning No-No Nanette?"

"Vaguely." I needed a notebook to keep track of all these random names.

"Well, her first husband was Augustus Paul Davidson Senior. They were the proud parents of Augustus Paul Davidson Junior."

"So?"

"Junior, as they called him around here, was your father's best friend since their diaper days."

"Did Junior disappear with my dad?"

"No, he went on to be a very successful businessman and was the mayor here for a while. They were a prominent family, with almost as much clout as the Tinsdales."

"Why aren't there any around town?"

"The curse of only one child per generation. After Junior and his wife died, Augustus the Third caught the acting bug and moved to Los Angeles where he married an actress. I can't remember her name but she had a few screen credits. They had one son. No-No moved west to be closer to them."

"So, if the Davidson name is still respected, and if Porter, I mean Augustus the Fourth, has a connection to Braddocks Beach, why did he use an alias when he moved back to town?"

"That, my friend, is the seven-point-nine-million dollar question."

Chapter Twenty-Nine

I ended up ordering the Swiss steak with mashed potatoes drenched in onion gravy, and green beans, also drenched in onion gravy by the time Libby delivered the Styrofoam container with inadequate partitions to my house. Sam had a big salad with a side order of breadsticks drenched in garlic butter which smelled divine.

We were Libby's last delivery of the evening, so she joined us around Aunt Izzy's table while we ate. After only two days, color had returned to her cheeks and pride had returned to her posture. We talked and laughed and had an enjoyable time, avoiding the topic of murder while we ate.

But as soon as dinner was over, we got to work. All of us.

The basement to my house was the stuff of which horror movies are made. I'd only been down there once, and only long enough to see my first mouse and then I'd gone back upstairs and locked the door. But this is where Aunt Izzy, in fact generations of Tinsdales, had stored their stuff, and as far as Sam was concerned, had to be the location of the Aunt Izzy's infamous chocolate chip cookie recipe.

The basement walls were made of painted river rock, original to the 1870s-era home. The floor was a twentieth-century wood, covered with a few decades worth of dirt. There were three rooms, each one illuminated by one naked, overhead light bulb. Each room had makeshift shelves, stuffed with all shapes and sizes of Tupper Totes. We could be down here for years.

We started in the front room, with Libby and me pulling down totes and peering in and poking through them while Sam kept herself busy checking messages on her cell phone. After twenty minutes, all we'd found in the containers was broken and rusted household junk and mildew-y clothes and other stuff that should have been carted to the junkyard a long time ago.

"Listen to this," Sam said as Libby and I poked through another tub of junk, with nary a cookbook or recipe to be found. "Scootch McKenzie over at B of BB said that they do hold the account for the church building fund, and quite a few checks had been cashed against the account lately, but she didn't have the payee information handy."

Sam's cell phone buzzed, announcing that another text message had just come in.

"Lawson over at Chase Bank said that Porter'd inquired about a safety deposit box on Wednesday but didn't sign up for one, let alone access one."

Which meant that ticket was floating around Braddocks Beach somewhere.

"That reminds me," Libby said as she brushed a spider web off her face. "Buddy Clarke is the one who delivered lunch to Reverend Hammersmith that day he was killed. Tinky told me Buddy'd been paying for his lunch at the counter when Brandon came in and said his bike had a flat. Buddy said he was heading that way himself and would drop the lunch off."

I opened another tub and stared at the contents without really seeing anything. Pieces of the puzzle that would be the three seemingly unrelated deaths floated around in my mind, but none of them seemed to interlock with the next. I focused my thoughts to slow down and replay the events of the last few days. Making order out of chaos was not my strong suit, but I was willing to give it the old college try.

I took myself on a mental road trip back to when we'd first heard the gunshot that had taken Reverend Hammersmith's life. The killer couldn't have escaped without someone seeing him. Sam had run toward the office. I had run away. I'd crashed into Buddy Clarke at the point where the back hallway connected to the front hallway in what made the rectangle around the business offices. One of us had to have seen the killer. Or the person had hidden in plain sight and none of us had noticed. Who else had I seen there? No one came to mind. I moved onward.

Sam and I had been the last ones in the house, along with Buddy Clarke, before the explosion. Maybe Buddy had noticed something out of the ordinary that might incriminate the killer? I posted a mental yellow sticky to tell Sam we needed to talk to Buddy again.

The next significant incident was finding Porter Trawbridge dead in the back of his truck. Strangled. Ready to be buried so as never to be found. He'd just won a lot of money in the lottery. Buddy Clarke had witnessed the moment when Porter had learned he'd won.

Was it my imagination, or did Buddy Clarke seem to be the common thread running through this entire murderous tapestry?

Oh. My. Gawd. With an audible click, the puzzle pieces fell into place.

"Sam, would Buddy have had access to the building fund like Porter did?"

"I believe he and Porter were co-signers. Both had to sign any check over $500."

Inside my head I heard puzzle pieces click together and voilà... an image emerged. Buddy hadn't been running *into* the church, because I'd have seen him coming through the doors. No, he'd been running out, down the back hall and towards the front door when we'd collided. He'd just delivered the reverend's lunch and possibly Reverend Hammersmith had questioned him in regards to the millions missing from the building fund.

Buddy hadn't happened by to rescue Sam and me when we'd locked ourselves in the manse. He'd arrived under the pretense of needing building plans for a meeting, but he'd walked out with us, empty handed. He must have come to blow up the house, and whatever evidence that Reverend Hammersmith had against him, but we'd been there and foiled his plans. He must have gone back later to finish the dastardly deed.

Buddy had been with Porter when he'd taken the ticket to the safety deposit box and had spun the story that it had been locked up. But he and he alone knew that Porter was carrying around a piece of paper worth millions to whoever held it. Chief Lewis indicated that could very well be the motive for Porter's murder.

And now we knew that Buddy had been the one to deliver the reverend's final lunch to him. "You know what I'm thinking?" I asked Sam and Libby. "I think Buddy Clarke killed both Reverend Hammersmith and Porter Trawbridge."

I was met with blank stares.

Before I could fill them in on how I had reached that conclusion, the sound of footsteps on the basement steps sent my heart spinning like the blades of a Seahawk helicopter preparing for takeoff. I watched in horrified silence as first a pair of workbooks appeared, followed by a hand holding a Glock, and finally the man I knew and feared--Buddy Clarke.

Worse yet, he had an "I'm gonna kill all of you" expression plastered on his face.

"Put your hands where I can see 'em." Buddy's low, scratchy voice blended with his boots scritching against the dirt on the floor. He approached our little group at a pace of a hundred and two year old man with a walker. It did more to jangle my nerves than the gun pointed at Sam's heart.

Chapter Thirty

"Buddy," Sam said in the southern drawl she reserved for foreign dignitaries. "Tell me you did not kill Reverend Hammersmith."

"If I told you the truth, Ms. Greene, then I'd have to kill you. And I don't think any of us want that to happen."

"And Porter Trawbridge?" Her voice trembled on this question.

The boot scritching stopped when Buddy got close enough for me to smell toasted tuna sandwich on his breath. "Let's keep things simple, here. You hand over that lottery ticket and I'll let you live to go poking your nose in some other poor soul's business."

"What makes you think we have the lottery ticket?" Sam drawled, her hands planted on her hips, not up high in the air like mine.

Buddy waggled the gun in my direction. "That hoodie you're wearing, Ms. Tinsdale. It's Porter's, isn't it?

I nodded.

"I've been looking all over for it. Porter's final words were, 'Go Bucks.' Then he laughed. I went through all his Ohio State stuff in his house. No ticket. Then you show up wearing his favorite hoodie. Put two and two together, and that has me thinking the winning ticket's in a pocket there."

Without any conscious effort, my hands searched all the pockets, finally stopping on the iPod pocket on the upper left arm. I heard the distinctive sound of crinkling paper. I'd been carrying seven-point-nine-million dollars around and hadn't even known it. Talk about feeling like I was gonna have a heart attack!

"No sudden moves now. Take that hoodie off and hand it over."

"You won't get away with it," Sam said in the bossiest voice I'd ever heard her use. And trust me, Sam was the Grand Poobah of Bossy Voices. "Chief Lewis already knows it was the motive for Porter's murder, and when you go to cash it in they'll be waiting with handcuffs."

"Don't you worry about that, Ms. Greene. I have a plan."

Buddy wiggled the gun in my direction, which made me wonder if his plan included shooting us even if we did turn over the ticket. Maybe he was only waiting until I had the sweatshirt off, because if he accidentally shot the ticket and tore it to pieces, it wouldn't be worth the paper it was printed on.

"Hurry now." He slipped his finger from the safety position on the side of the barrel and slid it into the trigger hole.

A tickly, icky feeling radiated along every inch of the forty-five miles of nerve endings that serviced my skin. I swallowed back the vomit that gurgled behind my tonsils and forced myself not to let the blackness take over.

Buddy was speaking. "...two nosy bitches poking around in my business. When you stopped by to ask those questions, I realized where Porter's hoodie was. I've been looking all over for it."

"You trashed Porter's house, didn't you?" Sam asked

"I thought the ticket was there somewhere."

"You said Porter locked the ticket up in a safety deposit box over at Chase."

"I talked him into burying it in his backyard. Only he never got a chance to do that. My mistake was going to take a leak. He hid the ticket while I was gone and wouldn't tell me where. But eventually I coerced a confession. Now, I'd really hate to shoot you, Ms. Tinsdale, but I've gotta have that lottery ticket, so if you just hand it over nice and slow." He raised the gun and pointed it at me.

"You'll never get away with it," Bossy Sam said.

"Oh, but I will. I've got three hostages I can use for negotiating, with one being the Queen Bee of Braddocks Beach."

No way was I gonna be anyone's negotiation tool. But what else could I do? I mean, Buddy had a gun, and I had nothing.

I heard Libby, behind me, express a tiny mew of fear.

I shrugged the sweatshirt from my shoulders and it slipped down into the storage tub at my feet that I'd been searching through when Buddy had made his appearance. I reached down to pick it up, and at the same time wrapped my hand around the handle of a bag. A very heavy bag, I realized, when I tried to lift it. So now, I had a heavy bag and the element of surprise on my side. Odds were still on the gun, but I had to try.

With a banshee yell, I hauled the bag out of the tub and swung it round and round over my head, winding up like a cowboy getting ready to lasso a calf. I put all my weight behind it and swung it towards Buddy, who ducked. The bag continued in a circle, and on the backswing hit Libby on the head. I heard her hit the floor.

But momentum still had the bag circling over my head and, still screaming, I took one step towards Buddy. This time I had a direct hit, smashing Buddy right in the kisser. He rocked backwards.

On impact, the bag exploded, and about a thousand marbles clattered to the wood floor. I took advantage of Buddy being distracted and ran for help.

Halfway up the stairs I heard a gunshot, then Sam's scream. Then another gunshot. And then silence.

I raced through the kitchen and like a trained SEAL on

an obstacle training course, got past the washer and dryer combo, and escaped out the back door. An awkward leap off the porch had me landing with a barrel roll in the thick fescue grass. I rolled to my feet and raced down the dirt path that led through the hedge and into Sam's backyard.

George met me on his deck.

"What's wrong? What are you yelling about?"

I hadn't realized I'd been yelling. "Call nine-one-one," I yelled again, even though George stood only a few feet away.

"Sam?" he said, the look of concern almost breaking my heart.

"Basement. Killer. Gun."

He was off like a ballistic missile.

"No! George! He'll shoot you too." But my words were swallowed up in the cheerful melodies of the birds singing in the trees.

I raced in his house and used his kitchen phone to call for help. Pressing three numbers was a challenge with fingers that shook like a crack head's after two days in rehab. It took four attempts and wasted precious time.

"Nine-one-one. What's your emergency?"

I couldn't form my words around the thing I most feared--that Sam lay bleeding to death in the basement of my house while Buddy Clarke tried to use her and Libby as a negotiating tool for freedom. I did manage to get out "Hostage. Basement. Gun. Blood. Dead. Hurry. Please." The first tears escaped and dripped down my cheeks. Soft, silent tears of one who has witnessed the horrors of greed and the total disregard for human life and felt helpless to make things right.

It seemed an eternity before I heard the sirens, but soon every emergency vehicle Braddocks Beach owned careened down Charleston Avenue, completely blocking the street. I raced out Sam's front door and motioned for the leader of the pack to follow me to the back of my house. I had just started my explanation--which wasn't any more coherent than my 911 call--when we rounded the corner to the back yard. What we saw froze the entire contingent in their tracks.

George walked down the steps of the back porch, carrying Sam's lifeless body. Her left arm looked like it had been attacked by a bear, as it was bloody and shredded all to pieces. Libby, her head bleeding from a temple wound, walked behind them holding Buddy's gun.

Officer Compton stepped from behind me, his gun drawn and focused on Libby. "Lay the gun on the ground, Ma'am, and step away."

"No, you don't understand," I said, but was shushed when another police officer tackled me and pulled me behind the garage. When I caught the breath that had been knocked out of me, I shoved the policeman out of my way and marched back out into the open. Libby had laid the gun on the ground, and George had laid Sam on the grass. I saw blood pouring from her arm, but her eyes were bright. Using her good arm, she frantically motioned me over.

I approached, the tears flowing harder with every step I took. When I was close, Sam held out her good hand. I took it and felt a piece of paper being pressed into my hand. The lottery ticket.

"Make sure that gets in the right hands," she whispered.

A policeman poked his head out of the backdoor and yelled, "He's alive but in bad shape. Get the paramedics down here stat."

Buddy Clarke was still alive. Good. Then I'd have the satisfaction of killing him myself.

Chapter Thirty-One

On the spectrum of things I hate to do, visiting a hospital rates a negative 110. The smell of rubbing alcohol makes me lightheaded; the hushed whispers make my heart skitter; and the machines beeping away a person's final seconds of life just plain make me want to run screaming for the hills. But the idea of dead bodies on ice in the basement morgue is the stuff that really makes my neck hair stand at full attention.

The sight of Sam laying there, helpless and weak, took the breath right out of me. She had more IV tubes than I could count and one of those damn machines that beeped.

I swiped at the moisture pooling on my upper lip. I had to be brave for her. "Hiya, Sam," I said in a voice reserved for playing Marco Polo at the swimming pool.

George, standing guard at Sam's bedside, snapped a finger to his lips and shushed me like I've never been shushed in all my forty-seven years and eleven months on this earth.

"Sorry," I said, throttling back to my library voice, which still echoed in the sterile room. "I would have been here sooner, but I didn't have a car."

"Did Titus get your Freelander fixed?"

"Not even close. Veralee let me borrow hers." I had to promise her first crack at Aunt Izzy's Christmas Cherry Kiss cookie recipe, but since I am officially out of money I had to resort to the long-lost custom of bartering. Wouldn't it be great if I could find a whole treasure trove of Aunt Izzy's secret recipes? Maybe I would write a cookbook to sell and make myself a fortune. Then again, I'd probably have to kitchen test the recipes myself, and that would pose a huge challenge, and probably pose a threat to life and limb for the entire neighborhood. But that was another problem for another day. Right now I was worried about Sam getting better. "How bad does it hurt?" I asked, with proper Queen Bee concern.

Sam shrugged in a way that said, *Not so bad* but laid her good hand over her bandaged arm in a way that said, *It hurts like hell.* She nestled deeper into the stack of white pillows, which took on a yellow tone compared to the color of her skin. The doctor had assured me that the ghost-white skin tone wasn't unusual for a woman who had recently undergone a seven-hour surgery. They'd had to pin her humerus back together. She'd lost a lot of blood.

George stood at her bedside as he'd done for the past two days, if my sources could be trusted.

"George, honey," Sam said in a voice so weak it made my stomach hurt. "I've a thirst for a cold tea. Would you be a dear and run down to the cafeteria and get me one please? Peach Snapple, if they have it."

"I don't think it's a good idea for me to leave you alone with Ellery just yet." George threw an angry-bear glance in my direction.

"I don't even want to think about all that unpleasantness. Ellery will catch me up on the Braddocks Beach gossip and it will be the best medicine in the world. Really."

George brushed a few blond curls from her forehead and touched his lips to her pale cheek, then turned and looked at me over his shoulder. "Ellery, you promise not to upset her?"

I snapped to attention and made my Girl Scout two-fingered promise symbol. I had no more desire to rehash the past few days than he had for Sam to hear it.

George rolled his eyes, then turned his attention back to his dearly beloved.

I looked away while they smooched.

As soon as the door clicked shut after George, Sam said, "I swear, if I have to send him for one more Snapple I'm gonna break one of those glass bottles over his head. But it's the only way I can get him out of the room long enough to get some news in here."

I laughed and approached Sam's hospital bed. "Well, I have some good news. Libby found an old recipe box in one of those storage tubs and there were two chocolate chip cookie recipes which she sent over to Polly to try out."

"That recipe box could be worth a gold mine. The Tinsdales were known for their culinary talents."

"That gene is not on my DNA, I'm sure. I can barely boil water for mac and cheese." We both laughed, because Sam had tried to teach me to cook and all efforts had been discarded, unfit for even canine consumption. "Speaking of old Braddocks Beach families, any idea why Augustus came back to town as Porter?"

"Oh, yeah. I gave No-No a call under the pretext of needing her address so I could send a sympathy card out. She told me Augustus had a bit of trouble with the law, drugs and theft and jail time and such, and he didn't want to bring that dirty laundry back to town where the Davidson name still garnered respect. Not sure why he came back though. And I'm not sure No-No really knew what she was talking about. She might have had him confused with Augustus the Third, who got into drugs really bad out in Hollywood. We'll probably never know the real reason."

Sam's good arm appeared from beneath her blanket and aimed a remote control at the television over my head.

"Coming up after the break..." The clear, measured words of a news anchor filled the room. *"...an arrest has been made in the string of murders that has recently plagued the lakeside resort of Braddocks Beach."*

I turned so I could see the TV. Buddy Clarke's face filled the screen, larger than life. I shuddered at the memory of him pointing the gun at my face.

"I hear Buddy's going to live." Sam filled me in on the details of his medical condition that could only be gleaned through inside sources. Hard to believe her gossip tentacles reached all the way up to the Medina hospital. "He blew a hole in his side when he slipped on the marbles rolling all over the floor. His first shot caught me, and the second one went off when he landed on the gun."

I shuddered at the mental image. All that blood. In my basement. Even though it had been professionally cleaned (by a commercial venture out of Cleveland that dealt in horrifying crime scene clean up--who'd a thunk?), it still was unsettling.

"Tell me how you figured it out." Sam strained to sit up and be alert.

Even though I'd promised George I wouldn't, I felt a need to unburden my thoughts to somebody. I pulled the side chair close to Sam's bed and leaned in so she could relax against the pillows and still hear every word I spoke.

With the first utterance, the floodgate holding back the horrific memories opened, and I blathered on what I'd figured out, relived those horrible moments in the basement, and ended my soliloquy by blubbering like an orphaned child when I got to the part when I thought she might be dead.

Sam used her good hand to stroke my head pillowed against her shoulder. "Hand me the phone there," she cooed.

"What?"

"The phone. Right there. I need to waylay George."

I reached for the corded phone on the stand a few feet from her bed and handed the receiver to her, dialing the numbers she recited from memory. "Mystic? Sam here. I need a favor. Can you call the hospital and have George paged and keep him distracted for five minutes? Ellery's explaining how she solved things, and I promise you an exclusive if you do this. Thanks, you're a dear. One question, any idea what Buddy did with all the money he embezzled from the building fund?" Sam listened and didn't so much as bat an eyelash. "That's interesting. He seemed like such a nice guy, but you never can tell what baggage the Newbees bring to town with them. Thanks. Bye, now." Energy wise, the old Sam was back.

I sniffed back the still trickling tears, drew a shaky breath, and honked the mucus into a Kleenex snagged off Sam's bedside table.

Sam gave me a *Queen Bees don't blow their noses like elephants* look, and I knew she was on the road to recovery.

Sam filled me in on her conversation. "Mystic told me Buddy Clarke was from Chicago, not Buffalo as he'd led us all to believe. Turns out he had a big time gambling problem. He'd been skimming money off various construction projects and betting on everything from the ponies to NFL games. He even, on occasion, paid back what he'd borrowed." Sam used her good hand to finger-quote the term. "Two weeks ago he'd taken a huge chunk from the church fund and gone down to Atlantic City and lost it all. Then Porter hit the lottery numbers, and Buddy figured he could use the winnings to replace the church's money, but then Reverend Hammersmith found out and confronted him. That's why Buddy killed the reverend. Then Buddy burned down the manse because he couldn't find the incriminating documents and he couldn't risk having someone else discover them."

"The killing trifecta; means, motive and opportunity."

Sam nodded.

George popped his head into the room, took one look at my tear-stained face and a storm cloud appeared over his head. "Ellery--"

His grumble was cut off when a nurse appeared at his side and interrupted him before he could work up a good head of anger. "There's an emergency phone call at the nurse's desk for you, Mr. Greene."

"What kind of emergency?" George looked skeptical.

"RJ has fallen—"

"Oh, dear God in heaven. If that boy hurt his pitching arm. Sam, honey, I got to take this. I'll be right back." George set six bottles of Snapple, in every flavor but peach, on Sam's bedside tray. "I won't be gone long, so you better talk quickly, Ms. Ellery, 'cuz I don't aim to leave you two alone again as long as I have breath in my body." With a finger-shake warning, he left the room.

Sam clicked the volume back on the TV.

"...the motive for Augustus Paul Davidson, aka Porter Trawbridge's murder appears to be over the seven-point-nine million dollar proceeds from July 11th Classic Lotto winning ticket. Questions remain as to how said ticket ended up in the hands of Braddocks Beach's societal leader Ellery Tinsdale after the shootout in her basement which injured a hostage and Clarke. It is also unclear who will collect the winnings. Miss Tinsdale is unemployed and without cash reserves herself, and yet has indicated she will turn the ticket and all its winnings over to Davidson's estate. Up next, the latest on demonstrations in the Middle East."

Sam hit the mute button again, then turned to me. "Good coverage on the murders, but it just goes to show you can't believe everything you hear on the news. Where did they get that part about you being broke? You've got the Tinsdale millions."

It was time Sam heard the whole story. I owed it to her. "Actually, Sam, I don't inherit anything unless I live here for five years. Aunt Izzy wanted me to become part of the community, and not take the money and run, so she put a few strings on the bequest. In the meantime, I've exhausted my personal savings, which weren't much to begin with, and have no income. So, I'm broke. Not even two pennies to my name and with your help I've run up debts all over town."

"Oh. My. Gawd. Why didn't you tell me? I've been spending your money like it was a bottomless pit."

The bedside phone rang. I lifted the receiver and handed it to Sam. "Greetings from hospital room three-one-three. Sure,

Max, she's right here." Sam held the phone in my direction.

"Morning, Max. Sorry I missed my appointment. Again. I'm here at the hospital visiting Sam. I'm sure you understand." I walked as far as the phone cord (no such thing as wireless handsets in a hospital) would allow toward the window, and looked out over the hospital parking lot. This sure was a busy place.

"No worries," Max said. "I'm calling to tell you your financial crisis is over. You and Sam will split the fifty-thousand dollar reward posted by the church for finding Reverend Hammersmith's killer. And then the church elders held an emergency meeting, and they've decided to award you a finder's fee for locating the lost lottery ticket and turning it over to Augustus Paul Davidson's estate. That's two hundred thousand, which should cover the tabs you've been running up all over town and leave you enough to get by for a while, if you're frugal."

I rested my forehead into the vee of my hand. That was the best news I'd had in a month. Maybe my whole life. But having learned that *Queen Bees Don't Show Their Emotions*, I tamped down my elation and spoke into the phone. "Thanks, Max. I appreciate the call."

After Max told me he managed to get an extension on the offer to purchase the property where Sam and I had been stranded--the place where we'd found Porter's/Augustus's body, we disconnected. Did I want to see the area turned into a housing development or keep it the way nature intended? I could maybe turn it into a public park in his name. But I was in no condition to make big decisions right now. I had two weeks to decide.

I gave Sam the update.

She smiled. "All's well that ends well, I guess."

"Not well for everyone. Your arm's been shattered, three people are dead, Scott, Melissa and Bing's lives are in shambles and the manse is nothing more than a pile of cinders."

"But we caught that guy who killed somebody in a hit and

run, Buddy Clarke is behind bars, and the winning lottery ticket was found, all thanks to our efforts. And Libby's life is back on track. She's moved into one of the cabins and Chiquita sent some clothes her way."

"I hope not designer. I can't afford to clothe both of us."

"I'll use my share of the reward money, don't worry. We make quite a team, don't we?"

Sam held out her fist, but instead of tapping her knuckles with mine as we've always done, I wrapped my fingers around her fist. She opened her hand and our fingers knitted themselves together in a show of friendship and solidarity.

"Speaking of thanks," I said. "I heard back from my friends in Virginia Beach that the picture frames for the McDougal's homecoming were a huge hit. Another ship wants us to make some for them. We could go into business or something." I smiled. If anyone had predicted I would ever want to go into business with Sam, I would have told them they were loopier than a box of Fruit Loops.

"I'd like that." Sam returned my smile, gave my hand a squeeze, and then released it. "But I haven't fulfilled my end of the bargain yet. I still owe you your Grandmother Gertrude's journals. And I have bad news on that front."

"What? You didn't do anything illegal, did you?"

"Not me personally, no. But my associate, managed to get to the vault, and I'm sorry to say it was empty."

"Are you telling me the journals never existed? And all that attempt to break in ourselves and getting caught up in Reverend Hammersmith's murder was for nothing?" I sunk down onto the bedside chair and drew a few deep breaths.

"No, those journals exist. I'm telling you that someone beat my associate there. So it seems we have a new mystery on our hands. We'll find who took them. It'll be simple enough."

Except nothing ever turns out as simple--or as safe--as Sam predicts.

If you missed the first Ellery and Sam cozy, here is a sample of how it all started...

THE BLOND LEADING THE BLOND

A Blonds at the Beach Mystery Series
Book One

Chapter One

The hounds of hell were hot on my heels.

Well, one hound, anyway. And the small, white terrier wasn't so much on my heels as snapping like a crocodile at the side pocket of my jacket as it billowed behind me. I had flashbacks of my fourth birthday party where a Rottweiler had ripped my arm to shreds. Premonitions of the terrier's teeth tearing into my jugular pushed me into survival-of-the-fattest mode.

Lifting my knees to my chest, pointing my chin towards the heavens and pumping my arms like the connecting rods on a steam locomotive, I raced around the circumference of a circle-shaped town park that appeared more accustomed to stroller-pushing moms and ice cream cone-licking tourists than a crazed woman being chased by a demonic canine.

I heard the dog's owner call from behind, "Pipsqueak

Rapscallion Zucker. Come here right now or no treats for you tonight, and I mean that."

The threats fell on deaf doggie ears.

I stumbled, now listing portside with the added weight of the mongrel attached to my pink-bisque pinstripe blazer. Brand-new, I might add, and its purchase had exhausted my annual clothing budget.

I swatted in the dog's general direction, my hand brushing across a cold, wet, snarling snout. Glancing down, I saw his little back paws paddling in the air as he flew behind me like an experienced parasailor. A parasailor with tiny, white piranha-like teeth. For lack of a better plan, I turned my attention forward, my legs pumping faster as I raced along, hoping the dog would fall off before my lungs exploded from my chest. Judging by the current level of pain throbbing beneath my breastbone, I'd be down in less than half a lap.

"Pippy, you're being a very bad boy. Very bad. Now come to Mommy."

The voice seemed much closer than it had on our trip past the gazebo. I glanced back again and, in doing so, broke the first rule of running, which also happens to be the first rule of life: Always look where you're going.

The next thing I knew, my irresistible force smacked into an immovable human object and down we went. The weight of yet another person landed on top of me, leaving me sandwiched between one wriggling, semi-squishy body beneath me, and one squirming, boney-elbowed body on top of me. The terrier tugged and snarled at my pocket like a seagull on a discarded peanut butter sandwich. Small comfort that he wasn't the least bit interested in shredding my flesh.

Amidst a symphony of groanings and grumblings, we unpiled from the pile-up and from my worm's eye view, I took a good look at the dog's owner. The woman exorcising the terrier from my pocket couldn't weigh more than 95 pounds. Dripping wet. She was a well-seasoned citizen, judging by her tight blue curls and cheeks that had given themselves up to gravity, yet she'd out-sprinted me. Pathetic.

"Ma'am? Are you okay?"

Good question. I rolled to a semi-sitting position and tried to catch my breath while conducting a quick mental inventory of all my 2,000 body parts. Sore knees, dirt under the fingernails, Jackie-O sunglasses askew, and an unnatural breeze along my upper thighs. I did my best scootch-and-tug until the hem of my skirt returned to a respectable level. It's not my nature to reveal so much of myself. Especially to strangers.

I looked around me. There were more strangers than I cared to count, pressing in an ever-tightening circle. The curiosity seekers wore identical expressions feigning horror while concealing amusement. I recoiled against the sea of camera phones pointed in my direction. So much for sneaking unnoticed into and then out of the town founded by my many-generations-removed grandfather. Then again I don't often get away with sneaking on account of my size. I measure in at a smidgen over six feet and my weight, well, let's just say I stopped monitoring it when my scale kept insisting I'd crossed the two-hundred-pound mark. And now, on account of my screaming and running, it seemed as if the entire town had taken notice of my arrival.

As if a band director had just lowered his baton, the whispers began. I picked up snippets of conversations.

"Could that be Ellery Tinsdale?"

"I read in the Bugle she was dead."

"She has the Tinsdale mouth."

"Look at those hands. I would think someone of her lineage would take more care of her appearance…"

"I expected a much younger woman. She looks eligible for a Golden Buckeye card…"

Ouch. That hurt. I'd always looked older, and wiser, than my years. I'd purchased my first six-pack of Pabst Blue Ribbon by age twelve without even so much as a raised eyebrow from the convenience-store clerk. I'd never fought nature and wore my blonde-fading-to-gray hair and curse-of-a-sun-worshiper wrinkles as a banner of honor, yet I'd been mistaken for a person eligible for social security benefits. AARP hasn't even made contact with me yet, and I didn't expect to hear from them for at least another 10 years.

"Ma'am?" the woman asked again.

"I'm fine." I leveled my gaze at the dog held by its owner still within jugular-piercing range. Pipsqueak stared at me and licked his chops. I put my hand to my neck, tucking thumb and forefinger close against my pulse points.

"I must apologize for Pippy, here." The woman shoved the frothing beast so that we were nose to nose. So close that I could feel his steamy breath and smell the remnants of the three-day-old carcass he'd had for lunch. Before I could recoil, his tongue snaked out and licked the tip of my nose.

A chorus of "Awwws" rippled through the crowd. Not an "awww" moment from my perspective. I scrubbed the doggie germs away with the back of my hand.

The woman tugged Pipsqueak back into the crook of her arm and patted his head. "The only time he ever acts that way is when a hamburger is involved." Her voice slid two octaves up the diatonic scale as she spoke. She twisted the dog so that they could kiss, Eskimo-style. "He wuves his hamburgers, wes he does. Wes he does." After some unintelligible doggie babble, she looked back at me and beamed like a proud momma. "He's acting as if you were wearing Eau de Big Mac perfume or something." The crowd laughed at her joke.

I didn't, but understood the unprovoked attack. Being on a new half-diet (eating half of the usual amount of my favorite foods), I'd tucked the uneaten portion of my triple-decker bacon-cheddar burger away. Crinkling the paper a few times since lunch served testament of my willpower. I hadn't been nearly as successful with the French fries...

Reaching into my pocket, I extracted the long-gone-cold half-burger and handed it to Pippy's owner. "He must have smelled this."

She took the proffered wad of foil and unwrapped it. Pipsqueak vibrated like a tuning fork as she did so, then wriggled himself free before the wrapper hit the ground. One bite and it was gone. Maybe it was a trick of the light, but I think the dog winked at me while licking ketchup and beef juice from his whiskers.

His owner beamed at me as if I'd just given her dog my last morsel of food, not my three-hour-old garbage.

"Let's break it up now, folks. Show's over." A man with a gun on his hip and a swagger to his gait began shooing away the crowd.

I'm no detective, not by any stretch of the imagination, but I suspected that the grass stains down the front of his white uniform shirt were because he was the poor soul I'd crashed into. I hoped assaulting a police officer while fleeing a hamburger-crazed dog wasn't a crime in Braddocks Beach, Ohio. I had no intention of spending a night in the pokey. In fact, I had no intention of spending a night in this town at all. I wanted to see the sights--which, judging by the dot on the map shouldn't take more than ten minutes--collect my token inheritance from an aunt I'd only heard of once as a child, and be heading back home to Virginia Beach in time to pack my bags for a month-long cruise to Alaska. I'd been planning and saving for it for three years. My ship sailed in two weeks. Three hundred and twenty-two hours, to be exact. Not that I was counting.

The crowd backed off but didn't disperse. The chatter became more frenetic and suppositional as I hauled myself, none too gracefully, to my feet. I started brushing yard debris from my clothes. My actions stilled as I caught the police officer's eyes, mere slits in a sea of scowling flesh and his bulbous nose sticking out like a Bozo's Bop Bag. Albert Bennett, Chief of Police, according to his nameplate.

"Ms. Tinsdale, I presume?"

Small towns. Gotta love 'em.

They had some secret radar that identified every stranger crossing the town's limits.

I stood a good six inches taller than the chief and used my height to trump his badge. I didn't like the way he'd said "Ms.", as if it left a bad taste in his mouth. "It's Miss Tinsdale," I said. I was proud of my single status. After more failed marriages than I cared to count, I'd vowed to remain a "Miss" for the rest of my life.

Chief Bennett's scowl tightened as he dipped his head. His hands assumed the position of authority, sliding to his belt. His left hand rested on the butt of his gun, his fingers fluttering against it as if his trigger-finger had an itch. Advantage: Chief Bennett.

"Miss Tinsdale," he said with all the friendliness of a cornered whistle pig. "Allow me to welcome you to Braddocks Beach. I hope you'll make time in your schedule to stop by the station and have a word with us. I have a few questions I'd like to ask you with regards to your aunt's murder."

I inhaled so quickly I feared the gaggle of Canadian geese waddling through the park would adopt me into their flock. But I wasn't alone in my surprise. Looking around, I realized word "murder" was just as much a shock to the crowd as it was to me. Aunt Izzy had been murdered?

"And don't think for a minute that just because your great-great-great-great-granddaddy founded this town that you'll get any sort of special treatment."

"Huh?" I always hated it when my third-grade science students "huh-ed" me, but it was the most intelligent thing I could think to say at that moment. What exactly was this man implying?

"You've got means," he said sizing me up and down. "And motive. All I have to do is prove opportunity and you'll spend the rest of your life looking through the steel bars of the Marysville Women's Reformatory. I hope you have a good alibi for the early morning hours of May thirtieth."

"Huh?"

ALL ABOUT JAYNE

Raised in a 150-year-old farmhouse in Chagrin Falls, Ohio, Jayne honed her story-telling skills at a tender age, convincing herself and others her home was haunted. She wove epic sagas of buried treasure guarded by spirits of slain pirates, and of the soul of a crazed ant locked in the attic, pacing the floorboards for all eternity.

Urged by her parents to forge a career in something that would enable her to be independent, Jayne dutifully went off and earned a B.S. in Accountancy from Miami University. She began her professional career as a CIA (not the sexy spy-thing, but a Certified Internal Auditor.)

But Jayne's parents did not foresee her marriage to a naval officer. Nineteen moves in conjunction with her husband's military career did not offer Jayne the stability she needed to climb the ladder to success, and when the box filled with her pinstripe suits was lost in one of those many moves, it seemed like an omen that it was time to make a career switch. So Jayne sat down and thought about what kind of job could be packed up and schlepped across the country at a moment's notice. *Aha*, she thought. *I can fulfill my lifelong dream of being a writer!*

Jayne's husband retired from the Navy and they are now "at anchor," in a cottage on the Chesapeake Bay, where she sells real estate by day and pens cozies by night.

Learn more about Jayne Ormerod (like why she writes under a nom de plume) at www.JayneOrmerod.com

Other Mysteries by Jayne Ormerod

NOVELS

The Blond Leading the Blond

Ellery Tinsdale's father never talked about his childhood, never once mentioned what happened to his family, and never ever gave any indication there existed a lakefront resort in central Ohio founded by his ancestors. Curious upon receiving notice of the death of an aunt she hadn't known existed, Ellery travels to Braddocks Beach in hopes of learning a bit about her heritage. There she finds she is to inherit the family house, the family jewels, the family real estate holdings, the family bank accounts, and, much to her dismay, the family role of Queen Bee. Ellery also finds herself accused of Aunt Izzy's murder.

Samantha Greene is the lifelong friend and neighbor of Isabel Tinsdale, as well as the self-appointed purveyor of Braddocks Beach history. The recent discovery of a surviving member of Braddocks Beach's 'royal family' sets the town abuzz with anticipation of Ellery's arrival. But Sam soon learns that Ellery is the only person to ever flunk out of Madame Rowena's School of Etiquette and has much to learn about making appearances, leading charity drives, heading up committees, and setting fashion trends. But first and foremost is the business of clearing the Tinsdale name of murder.

What do a third-grade science teacher and a small-town socialite know about tracking killers? It's what they don't know that may hurt them.

NOVELLA

Behind the Blue Door: 230 Periwinkle Place

Can you have a future if you can't remember the past? When Skye Crenshaw Whitmore is shown a picture of a house with a blue door, she recalls living there as a young girl. At first the memories are of the warm and fuzzy variety; little moments spent gardening or reading with her mother. Upon learning that the house on Periwinkle Place is where her mother died, darker memories bubble to the surface but fail to assemble into a complete picture. With more questions than answers, she sets off to find out what exactly happened in that house thirty years ago. Skye soon learns that old memories never die, they just wait...*Behind the Blue Door.*

SHORT STORIES

"Best Friends Help You Move the Body"
Virginia is for Mysteries anthology

Playing hooky from work lands two best friends in trouble when their day of sightseeing has them discovering only one thing…a dead body.

"The Tide Also Rises"
Chesapeake Crimes 3 anthology

A stay at a friend's house is not quite the get-away she'd hoped for when she discovers a dead body and gets involved in finding the killer.

"When We Were Middle Aged and Foolish"
Available as a Free Read on Jayne's Blog
www.JayneOrmerod.Blogspot.com
Just click on the FREE READ!!! Tab

The last thing Sydney and Monica Lynn expect to find in a stolen trash can is a dead body, especially when that trash can belongs to Monica Lynn's estranged husband.

Made in the USA
Middletown, DE
24 November 2018